SOMEWHERE FAR FROM HERE

BY

ALEXANDER J STRANSKY

Publisher: Alexander J Stransky
ISBN: 978-1-7354187-0-4

I was 21 years old when I finished writing this novel.

I was 22 years old when I decided to put it on the proverbial shelf, accepting that it would not see daylight.

For those struggling to find where they belong...

And for those willing to dust off a dream...

CHAPTER 1

My name is Greg Madison and I don't particularly like looking in the mirror. Senior year of high school is supposed to be one of the best years of a guy's life, but I guess that's only true if you're happy with your life. I don't want to go to school this morning, hell I don't wanna get up this morning. All the people I've grown up with seem to have some kind of focus in their lives. They all have something going for them: serious relationships, decent jobs, some kind of talent. They all seem to have their lives playing out pretty well. Some of them already know for sure what their plans are after graduation. Not me though, I can only handle it one day at a time. Compared to everyone else I feel pretty empty and directionless.

"Get up Greg! You can't afford to be late to school anymore," my father yelled. All right, shut up, it's only 7:25. I still have time. Geez, I can't even enjoy the morning without my father riding me. I staggered out of bed (no time for a shower this morning) and grabbed the jeans I'd been wearing for the past couple of days. I threw on an old Ramones t-shirt and headed downstairs.

I sat down at the table while my mom put down the food. My dad looked at me and said, "Y'know if you're late for math two more times you're gonna lose credit for that class?"

"Not like it matters, I'm not passing anyway," I said as I ate my toast.

"That's the problem with you Greg, you don't have any motivation." That's not true; I would have plenty of motivation if it was something that I cared about. I nodded my head to agree with my father. At least it would get him to stop talking to me. My dad had to leave early so he quickly finished his breakfast and got up. "I hope you do good at school today Greg," he said as he patted my shoulder.

"Yeah, I'll try." He turned toward my mom.

"I'll be back a little earlier tonight and we'll go out to dinner like we planned."

"Sounds good hon," she replied. Yes! No one to bother me tonight, I would have the house to myself.

"See ya dad," I said as he walked out the door.

Don't get the wrong idea, I don't dislike my parents, they just get on my nerves a lot. My father can be pretty strict. Sometimes it feels like he never gives me a moment to breathe. He wants me to do real good on everything. That's a noble idea but it just isn't gonna happen. I don't know if he quite understands that. It's like I can't have any imperfections because it's gonna bring him down too, or something.

I was left alone with my mother in the kitchen. She's not bad either but she just doesn't understand me. She dislikes most of the things I'm into. She thinks I waste too much time on useless stuff. I listen to a lot of heavy metal and punk and she thinks it's all garbage music, although she doesn't care to know enough about it to make that decision reasonably. After she cleared the table I got up to get going. "You're gonna wear those crummy jeans again," she asked as she looked down at the holes forming in the knees.

"These pants are fine," I snapped back.

"What, is that how those there Ramones wear their pants? Just because they look like a bunch of bums doesn't mean you have to. That's a stupid style," she declared.

"Yeah, that's what you think," I said. Man, just leave me alone already. "All right, I have to go, bye."

"Ok. Take care."

I got my book bag and walked out the door. I hopped into my beat up old Nissan. It was pretty cold this October morning and it didn't help that the heater in my car didn't work. I cursed myself for not bringing a jacket. Oh well, I didn't have time to go back in; I had to get to school on time. As I fired up the engine I slid in Metallica's "Black Album", one of my favorites. Seemed so long ago since I first got it. Crap, it's already 7:40. I resigned myself to the fact that I had five minutes to get to school.

In case you were wondering, yes, I was late. I was hoping to slip into math class and sit down without incident but that wasn't Mr. DeBurns' style. I walked in and got about halfway to a desk before DeBurns spotted me. "Mr. Madison, how nice of you to join us." I don't know exactly why but this guy just didn't seem to like me. I never did anything to him but he seemed to enjoy giving me a hard time whenever he could.

"I'm sorry," I muttered.

"Gregory," he was using my full name, which I rarely go by, "it's very easy to do something someone doesn't appreciate and then say you're sorry. I mean, I guess that's what I'll say when I have to give you an F." Here he goes again, trying to put me down in front of the class. "So what was it this time, was there a deal with your burnout friends in the parking lot?" Hey jackass, my friends aren't burnouts! None of us smoke up more than once, or maybe twice a month. Or, well...

"Mr. DeBurns I don't think that you –"

"Sit down Greg," he cut me off in mid-sentence. "One more late and you automatically fail, remember that, one more." I was pissed off. I gave him a stare that let him know and he gave me one back. "Now getting back to problem six…" he continued his lesson. Man, what a scumbag. He has to give me problems, probably cause he's unhappy with his own life and that's how he makes himself feel good.

I didn't talk for the rest of the period. I just sat there, stewing in my anger, thinking about what bad things could possibly happen to Mr.

DeBurns between now and tomorrow. The bell finally rang and I got the hell out of there, not stopping to listen to whatever reminder he was giving to the class. I made my way down the hall and disappeared into the faceless mass of people.

I looked around and noticed how crowded it was. Wow, so many people here – I wonder how many of them are actually happy and feel accepted? I passed by some jock football players. They were laughing and pushing each other, having fun. Yeah, they've got it going good. They're well known and they get to hang around with attractive cheerleaders. I looked the other way and I saw a bunch of preps. I don't get it. They walk around acting like they're better than everyone, showing off their new and expensive clothes, cars, and whatever else mommy and daddy buy them, and somehow they're popular? That makes no sense. I noticed a few nerds entering the library. Even they, who aren't really looked upon highly, seem to at least have a sense of belonging. They can usually be seen together in their tightly knit group, doing whatever it is that pleases them, like hi-tech computer junk or whatever, stuff that I don't particularly care for. I looked at the side of the hall and saw a couple hoods yelling out some insults to kids that were passing by. That's how they get their kicks, by giving others a hard time. They try to get each other's approval and respect by acting tough and sure, they are respected…by other asshole kids.

Then you had my group. I wouldn't call us outcasts but we were definitely separate, we did our own thing. We didn't show school spirit or participate in any activities. To us, school was more like a place to have something to do when you had nothing better; we had no problems ditching class for a good reason. We were a bunch of loners who occasionally drank a beer, smoked a joint, or got into trouble.

"Hey Greg!" I could tell by the voice who it was. I turned around to meet my best friend, Daniel Wells. He was clad in his typical uniform – either some Ozzy or other heavy metal band t-shirt, a pair of jeans, and an old, beat up army jacket his uncle had given him. We had been best friends for nearly our entire lives. Daniel was the only person who truly understood me and we were always there for each other, no matter what. We knew each other inside and out. Standing next to him was my other dear friend Tiffany Warner, who also became his girlfriend this year. I liked Tiffany a lot; she was such a sweet girl. Although I had never been attracted to her I still thought she was beautiful nonetheless. She was wearing her black cargo pants, a plain white t-shirt, and her green bandana. Although we were good friends, Tiffany didn't know my deepest emotions and insecurities. I always kept myself in a good mood whenever I was around her because I liked her so much.

"Hey guys," I greeted them.

"Hi Greg, what's going on," Tiffany asked me.

"I don't know, nothing much. DeBurns was being a prick to me."

"Yeah I hate that guy," Daniel chimed in. "Well if you wanna do something fun, me and Tiff are going to the movies after fourth period, you wanna come?" Hmm, go to the movies with my friends or stay in school on a day that already started on a bad note? I love movies; they give me a chance to just get away for a while. Wasn't much of a contest. See, this is one of those reasons for cutting class I was talking about.

"Yeah, I'll go," I answered. After a few more minutes of small talk I decided to leave. While I was on my way, I saw in the distance a girl who was in one of my classes, chemistry to be precise. Her name was Kate Berline and she was fairly decent looking. I talked to her a few times, but nothing significant, I didn't really know her. I would love to get together with her. It actually wasn't too farfetched of an idea. She wasn't popular and I never really saw her hanging out with other guys too often. Maybe if I talked to her more, got to know her, something could happen between us. I watched her head into one of the buildings and I snapped back out of my fantasy. I headed to my next class, killing time until fourth period ended.

When it was time to leave I snuck out to the parking lot, looking out for any teachers or other authority figures. When I decided it was clear I met Daniel and Tiffany there. We piled into Daniel's car, keeping an eye out for anyone, and zipped out of there before anyone could see us.

CHAPTER 2

6:42 p.m., wow 7 o'clock just can't come fast enough. It was another typical day at Rexmon Clothing. What's Rexmon? Oh, that's my go nowhere job. I make minimum wage and that probably won't change anytime soon. I've been here about eight months and over that period of time I've steadily grown more indifferent toward the actual work. It's just that it is sooo repetitive. Unload this, set up that, check on this, and so on. I find my mind wandering a lot when I'm not talking to my boss, Nancy.

Nancy is in her mid-forties and has been in this business for quite a while. She's pretty nice and seems to genuinely care about me. I usually asked her advice whenever I needed an adult opinion. "What are you going to do tonight, Greg," she asked.

"I don't know, I don't have any plans, maybe just relax in front of the TV," I replied.

"Easy there, don't strain yourself," she joked. Ha, that made me chuckle.

"Hell, it beats doing inventory, like you're gonna be doing in a few hours – without me I may add."

"Don't remind me, those boxes of coats are already getting on my nerves." Just then the door opened and another customer moseyed in. "He's all yours," she told me. Great. I went up to him and began my usual spiel. "Hi, how are you doing, can I help you with anything?"

"No thank you, I'm just looking," he casually stated. Yup, that was the typical answer. Seems like people don't like being bombarded with salesmanship as soon as they walk into a store. Whatever, I didn't care. I was just doing my job the way Nancy trained me. I went back to my area and occupied myself by looking at some catalogs for a while.

Well, 7 o'clock finally rolled around. Excellent. "All right Nancy, looks like it's time for me to hit the bricks, take care, I'll see you on Thursday."

"Goodbye Greg, have a good night."

I stepped out into the cool air of the parking lot. Just then my phone rang. I took it out and saw that it was Tiffany. Cool, I hadn't hung out with her in a few days. "Hey Tiff, what's going on," I answered.

"Hi Greg. What are you doin?"

"Nothing, just got out of work. What's up?"

"Do you wanna go to the mall?"

"Who else is going," I asked.

"No one, just me and you."

"Yeah, what's Daniel doing?"

"He's with Johnny, they're going to a show." Oh yeah, that's right. He was going to check out this new local band. He told me about it but I didn't feel like going. Well, he got Johnny to go with him. Johnny Brewer was my other good friend. I'd known him just as long as I knew Daniel. He was a fun guy and a pretty good person but the only thing was that I never felt that we were as open to each other as I could be to Daniel or Tiffany.

"Yeah, sure, I'll go with you. I'll be by your house in a half hour," I said as I gave her a goodbye.

I pulled up to Tiffany's house and met her at the door. "Hi Greg, just give me a few minutes, ok," she said.

"No prob'," I responded. I chose to wait outside and soaked up the cool night breeze. The wind chilled right through my shirt but it felt good in strange way. She came back out and I walked her to my car, opening the door for her in the process. I then got in and started up the Nissan, or "Barely Reliable", as I liked to call it.

I liked spending time with just the two of us. Don't misunderstand me though, this wasn't out of any type of shiftiness towards Daniel and their relationship. After all, this was my best friend's girlfriend. But the fact was that I didn't have many female friends, let alone feel liked and appreciated by tons of girls like some guys I knew. Tiffany made me feel good just by being around her.

We had plenty of laughs during the night and enjoyed ourselves. When we were leaving the mall we bumped into a few acquaintances from school, this guy Steve and his girlfriend, Cindy, along with her younger sister. We weren't great friends with these people but we would talk if we saw each other out in public. We BS'd with them for a little bit. I asked Steve how he was doing on the football team. "Yeah man, I made it to the number three wide receiver, hell yeah," he excitedly proclaimed. Personally I didn't care that much but at least this guy was happy.

"So yeah what have you guys been up to," Cindy asked.

"Well I'm still working my ass off at Lex's Diner," Tiff replied.

"How 'bout you Greg, you play drums right," Cindy asked. My drums, damn I hadn't played those in months. My parents bought me them at my request but they also had their reasons. They hoped that if I wasn't going to participate in anything at school I might as well have some sort of creative outlet. I'd been playing them for about six months and they were fun at first. However, just like everything else in my life, I never became good at them so I got discouraged easily and soon lost interest.

"Yeah, I'm doing all right on my drums but I'm taking it slow," I lied. I didn't want people I didn't know all that well to find out I was a quitter. Besides, maybe I'd start playing again if I got motivated, who knows? We talked for another five minutes or so.

"Y'know you two look like you'd make a good couple," Steve declared.

"Yeah," Tiffany began jokingly, "he's my second boyfriend." We all had a good laugh at that. Oddly enough though, and sadly too, Tiffany was the closest thing I ever had to a real girlfriend. I always had problems with girls. I didn't know what the hell to do. I was so damn unconfident and nervous when it really came down to it. I had gone out on a few dates with a couple of girls here and there but I was never actually interested in any of them. I just did it as a service to someone else usually. It seemed as if no girls who I ever would have considered getting together with actually liked me.

After a little more meaningless conversation, Tiff and I decided to leave. I drove her to her house and got out to walk her to the door. "It was fun tonight Greg, thanks for dropping me off."

"Yeah, no problem. You know I'd do anything for you because I loovve yoouu," I said in that goofy way that always made her smile.

"Good night Greg," she responded in her high-pitched, equally goofy way as she hugged and kissed me goodbye.

"Good night, take care," I said as I turned to leave. You know, come to think about it, that's all I really wanted in a girl. Just someone I could enjoy talking to and could hold for a little bit. I walked back to my car feeling both a little happy and a little sad.

CHAPTER 3

"Ok, Greg and Johnny, you're up after Tim and Rob if there's enough time today," stated Mrs. Cooper.

"Yup, no problem," replied Johnny. Yeah, no problem my ass. Me and Johnny had to give our report on the history of the electric chair in front of the class and we weren't even close to done. It was fifth period history and there were approximately eight minutes to kill. Man, I hoped these guys took a long time. "Yo Johnny," I whispered, "if we have to, we better ask them questions when they're done to stall a little longer."

"Yeah, you bet your sweet ass," he replied with a smirk on his face. That was Johnny, always a goof, even under pressure situations.

"It's your fault we're not done," I stated. I recalled to him how we had spent the previous night with the intention of finishing the report and had decided to split a joint with the hope that it would help us relax enough to tackle the project. Instead we got distracted when we noticed that The Twilight Zone was on TV. Man, that show was even more out there when you considered our present condition. By the time we got done watching a few episodes we pretty much forgot about the report. We then spent the rest of the night reminiscing about things we did in the old days and things we hadn't done yet but spoke about as if we had already accomplished them. I accused him that he was responsible for us being in this situation.

"Hey, I offered it but you're the one who accepted," Johnny fired back at me. "If you didn't accept we wouldn't have done it."

"All right, shut up, you're right," I ended the conversation.

I was so relieved to hear the guys drone on about the Ford Motor Company. They used up just enough time for us to avoid having to go today.

"Very good gentlemen. Ok we'll end here today, Johnny and Greg you'll be first on Monday," Mrs. Cooper informed us.

"Oh that's too bad Mrs. Cooper, we really wanted to go today," Johnny said. Man, this guy is always on.

The bell rang and it was lunchtime. Finally, some rest and relaxation. Me and Johnny strode into the lunchroom and threw our junk onto our usual table. We sat down and guarded the fort while we waited for Daniel and Tiffany. A favorite time passing game of ours was something we called "Ugly, Decent, Hot". Basically, me and Johnny would study each girl that walked by and crudely label them ugly, decent, or hot. The game would grow more interesting whenever some girl overheard our comments about her. The highlight certainly had to be the time Dianne Maple overheard Johnny comment about how many beers he would need to ingest in order for her to move up to hot status. Well Johnny sure didn't need any alcohol to reach face slap status that particular day. "Ugly, ugly, hot, decent," I began as I surmised the cafeteria.

"Hot, ugly, decent, hot, decent, ugly," Johnny picked up.

"Hey Johnny," I stopped checking out girls for a second and got serious. "Do you know Kate Berline," I asked. Kate, the girl that I had a bit of a crush on and who was the sole reason I had any interest in chemistry.

"Yeah, I'm not friends with her but I know who she is."

"What do you think of her?"

"She's all right, she's not like spectacular looking or anything but she's not bad looking either."

"Well y'know how I said I've talked to her a couple times? Well today I actually had a conversation with her."

"Good job brother."

"You think she would have any interest in me?"

"Well let me tell ya," Johnny started, "first, you did good in not setting your hopes too high." Oh yeah, I could tell some sarcasm was to come. "You're the type of person who has to settle for certain things in life. You, my friend, have to take what you can get, y'know? You have to buy the dented car, the expired groceries, the defective merchandise, the –"

"Yo asshole, a simple yes or no would do." We couldn't help but start laughing. After he composed himself, Johnny told me to go for it. I saw her just paying for her lunch. Damn man, he's right. I decided to put myself on the line a little and invite her over to our table. "Hey Kate, you wanna sit over here?"

"Oh…yeah…okay," she replied after I caught her attention. She sat down and I introduced her to Johnny. We began talking about school and class for several minutes. We both had something in common – we disliked our chemistry class.

"Yeah that worksheet pack she gave us is killer, it's like almost a half inch thick," I exaggerated.

"Yeah I know right. I just don't have enough time to do it all. I have to work today."

"Where do you work," I curiously asked.

"Oh, the town Youth Club. I'm a lifeguard but it's really a joke of a job. All I have to do is tell the little kids not to do anything stupid."

"Do the little demons give you trouble?"

"No," she began, chuckling. Yes! I made her laugh a little. "I put some fear into them. If they start getting wild I tell 'em that I just might have to have a talk with their parents when they show up."

"Sounds like you do a good job." I small talked with her for a few more minutes before Kate said she had to go.

"Yeah, I have to go to the library and do some research now," she told me.

"Ok, I guess I'll see you around," I responded.

"Yeah, see ya."

Excellent. Today could be the first step towards possibly getting together with her. Eventually Tiff and Daniel joined us, fashionably late of course. "Sorry," Daniel began, "but Tiff wanted to grab something in my car – me."

"Oh yeah, real cute," I said.

"Yup, that's just what I wanna hear after eating lunch," Johnny agreed.

"So what's up," Daniel asked.

"Hey, you should've seen it," Johnny proclaimed, "Greg was buttering up some girl."

"All right man, I'm proud of you," Daniel said while smiling.

"What happened Greg," Tiffany asked.

"I just talked to this one girl who I have a class with. Nothing really happened."

"So what are you goin' to do about it," Daniel asked me. He knew full well I didn't have any kind of game plan in my mind.

"Dude I just talked to her for like ten minutes geez, you can't just go from barely knowing someone to trying to get all over them. It doesn't work that way," I countered.

"Well Greg," Tiff spoke up, "that could've been ten minutes of her wanting you, ya never know." They all started joking about my non-existent love life and how this girl could be "The One". After a while the bell rang and it was time to leave.

"All right, let's roll," Johnny said. "Hey Daniel, time to bust some skulls in dodge ball today, huh?"

"You know it," he answered. They went on ahead of us.

"Hey Greg," Tiff said to me smiling, "I hope this works out for you."

"Yeah I hope so too."

CHAPTER 4

"You'll be seated now gentlemen, right this way," stated our waitress as we proceeded to follow her for a short walk. I was starving and could not wait to sink my teeth into a finely cooked piece of meat. We had arrived at our favorite place to eat – 'Round the Clock Diner – about fifteen minutes ago and had been patiently waiting to be seated. Me, Daniel, and Johnny were having a guy's night out without Tiffany. Actually, she declined our invitation but that doesn't sound as cool. 'Round the Clock wasn't like a super nice place but as we walked I could feel that we raised a few eyebrows. These older folks probably thought we were a couple of hoodlums stopping for a meal before we would be up to no good.

I took a look at the three of us. We were all wearing boots and beat up jeans. I had on an Alice Cooper t-shirt with a denim jacket and a black beanie hat. Johnny had his leather jacket to go along with his unkempt hair. Daniel was wearing a blue bandana and a t-shirt with the comic book character Spawn perched on a city roof. No doubt some of the older folks thought we were troublemakers. I guess I could understand where these people were coming from after all. Oh well, you can't please everyone.

We took our seats and welcomed the ability to relax at the table. I gazed at the menu with delight while my friends chatted away. "Hey Johnny," Daniel began, "two bucks says you won't try to order a beer."

"You don't think I'll do it," he responded.

"That's why I'm betting." Ha. That should be fun to watch. "Hey, by the way, did you guys check out our waitress? Damn." He was right; the waitress in question was pretty attractive. Her hair was dyed a dark red and she had a great smile to go along with her sexy figure. She looked to be maybe a couple of years older than us.

"Yeah, she is hot," I confirmed.

"Well Daniel, five bucks says you don't make an honest attempt to get her phone number. And if you do get it I'll even buy you dessert," Johnny countered to Daniel's previous proposition.

"All right, I'll do it."

"Dude, you have a girlfriend," I pointed out.

"Yeah I know," Daniel explained, "I've been with Tiff for eight months but I just wanna see if I still got the skills y'know. It's not like this is serious, I'm not actually gonna call her. But by the way don't tell her about it. I don't want her to get pissed."

"Yeah, don't worry about it. This is me here," I assured him.

We chatted for a few minutes while waiting for our waitress, which from this moment on we referred to as Red. And speaking of Red here she came now.

"How are you guys tonight," she joyfully asked.

"Fine," replied me and Johnny casually. Daniel had other plans.

"Well I wasn't doing very good before, but now that I see we lucked out with such a pretty waitress I'm doing great." Wow, that was a ballsy line.

"Aw, well thank you," she replied with what I determined to be sincerity. She began taking our orders by asking us what we wanted to drink. When it came to Johnny he spoke as if he weren't the joker we knew him as.

"Yes, I would like a glass of Coors please." He sounded like he was trying to give off his most mature impression.

"Well," Red began, "I hate to be strict but I have to see your ID. I might not have asked you on any regular night but the boss has been telling us lately that we have to."

"Oh really," Johnny asked as he was poking through his jacket, I guess in an attempt to not look too stupid.

"Yeah, we had two kids come in here last week and they ordered a few drinks. I guess they were being disruptive, cause some customers complained about them. Turns out they were a little under twenty-one. Since then, the boss has been a bit more serious about checking IDs."

"Oh damn," Johnny said in mock surprise. "I think I left my driver's license in my other jacket. You don't think you could give me the drink though, I mean, I am twenty-one," he lied.

"Well you look like you could be but I'm not positive," Red responded. "I'm sorry but I can't." Johnny nodded.

"Yeah," interjected Daniel, "a sweet girl like you wouldn't want to break the rules. I'd hate to see you get in trouble."

"Oh really," she asked in a lighthearted way.

"Uh huh," he returned with a flirty smile. She smiled back at him and took the rest of our orders.

"Ok, I'll be back."

"Take your time," Daniel said to her as she left.

"Well I tried ordering the damn beer but they screwed me over with their legal mumbo jumbo," exclaimed Johnny.

"You did your best, kid," came Daniel's response as he threw two dollars in Johnny's direction.

"Hey man," I said to Daniel, "she didn't seem turned off. I'm pretty impressed."

"Well you just have to be confident…and remember, women love compliments." Well that sounded pretty sensible. Let me see though: compliments – yeah, in the right situation I could do that. Confidence – that was my downfall. I had little, if any. I'm usually filled with nervousness and dread when a friend tells me to go up to some random girl in an attempt to come on to her. I hated myself for that. Who knows how much better my life could have turned out if socializing hadn't always been such an obstacle?

So the rest of the evening continued with Daniel flirting with Red whenever she returned to our table. Daniel was fairly smooth with the ladies; I'll give him that. He usually had no problem attempting to talk to girls he considered desirable. Even if he wasn't as successful as he had hoped, he rarely got blatantly blown off, and when he did it didn't even seem to faze him. Therein lay his secret – he wasn't afraid of looking stupid because in his mind he was confident that girls liked him.

He had had a few somewhat serious girlfriends throughout high school. Now at eight months with Tiffany this had been his longest commitment. We had met Tiff freshman year in one of our classes and eventually she ended up joining our hangout group. Even back then they lightly flirted with each other in a jokeful way. Then last year they got together and now here we are – senior year in high school.

I looked over at Johnny's face and thought about his lifestyle. He was something of a partier, at least compared to us. He was usually the one to toss out the idea of getting drunk or possibly stoned when we hadn't had any excitement in a while. He never had a truly serious girlfriend – certainly never more than a few weeks. Why? Because he usually hooked up with girls he met at parties. These girls would sometimes last for a few weekends and after they both got what they wanted, ahem, laid each other a few times, they would eventually split up.

I wanted something more substantial than that. I know most guys my age are just interested in sex but I wanted to form a deep bond with a girl before I ever even thought about doing anything with her. I mean, a lot of people just throw around their sexuality like it's not a big deal. Yeah, Daniel and Tiffany regularly have sex but at least they love each other so that's fine in my book.

By the time the meal ended I was disgustingly full and had to go to the bathroom. Johnny came with me. On our way back to the table we saw Daniel talking to Red before she moved on to another section of the restaurant. The first thing he said to us as we took our seats was, "Here's the check. You might wanna look on the back." Johnny turned it over and I asked him what it said. He looked at me and responded, "Thanks sweetheart, give me a call. Jessica." And there was her number. Wow. Yes, I was in awe. I wish I had that kind of ability. With a huge grin on his face, Daniel spoke, "Hey Johnny, I'll have the pumpkin pie to go."

CHAPTER 5

Wow, I could not believe how great this party was turning out for me! I almost didn't go but then Daniel talked me into going, cause he didn't want to be there alone. As it turned out, Kate was here and, believe it or not, I'd been talking to her for a great deal of time, getting to know her better. We had been enjoying each other's company and when she decided to leave she asked me to come outside with her. I wondered what she had up her sleeve. I walked her to her car and it was then, without warning, that she leaned towards me and kissed me. I was shocked. It was unbelievable. It was incredible. It was…a dream? Son of a bitch! I slowly looked around and saw the familiar surroundings of my room. I lay there for a few minutes in disbelief. Man, it felt so real. Ugh, well I guess it's back to reality for me. What day was it? Saturday. Oh no, I have to go with my father to do some manual labor at some old lady's house today.

I decided to jump in the shower to start my day. I savored the warmth and comfort for a good ten minutes. As I got out I checked myself in the mirror. I need to get in shape. Well, I wasn't fat or anything but I could definitely stand to lose some pounds from my belly. All right, working out will go on my to-do list. As I got dressed I turned on the radio for a little bit of company. I was greeted by the deep and sadly melodious voice of Johnny Cash singing about some lost love. Cash, what an unbelievable life he lived. I wish my life could be a fraction as exciting as his was. Wait, what am I talking about? Having my dad boss me around for the next few hours should be exciting enough.

I put on an old pair of jeans that were my designated work pants. I didn't care if I got them dirty. I also put on my old, abused AC/DC "Highway to Hell" t-shirt. Hopefully my mom made something for breakfast cause I sure as hell didn't want to go work for a couple of hours without food in my stomach. Yes! I was in luck. She cooked eggs, waffles, and sausages. I excitedly sat down but before I even swallowed my first bite my mom questioned my choice of clothing. "Y'know Mrs. O'Leary is a pretty old lady," she said as she looked at me.

"So…" I could tell where this was going.

"Well I think she might be a little turned off by your shirt." The image on the shirt was a picture of the band, one of them had fake devil horns on his head, and on the bottom it said Highway to Hell. It wasn't as bad as it sounds. If you weren't paying attention you might not even notice the horns and it would look like any typical picture of a band. Also, the shirt was so messed up that the words Highway to Hell were cracking, so you had to take a few seconds to make it out.

"So what do you want me to do?"

"Put on a different shirt."

"What? I don't think it matters what I wear. I mean, I'm just going there to do physical work for her. She ought to be happy that we're doing her this favor in the first place; professional help would cost a lot more. She shouldn't care what I'm wearing."

"Well you're not wearing that shirt there, so go change." My mom was starting to sound pretty stern. We argued for a few more minutes until I decided to change the damn shirt so I wouldn't have to hear it from her anymore. I was mad, not necessarily because I had to put on a different shirt, it didn't really matter what I wore. No, it was the principle of the matter. I had to be forced to do things the way she wanted. It never ends with them; my parents are always screwing me over.

At this point I just wanted to leave so I began to go out the door to meet my dad. He was in the garage loading up the truck. Before I could get out the door I heard my mom say to me, "Hey, there's a whole plate of food here you didn't eat."

"I'm not hungry," I said bitterly as I closed the door behind me. I went to the garage and my dad greeted me, not with a mornin' or a how ya doin' like you might expect, but with a "You're late, now gimme a hand with these tools, I've been loading 'em all myself." I didn't say anything and just did as he instructed, putting things wherever he told me to. Yup, it was gonna be a great day.

I didn't say much during the car ride. I didn't want to be there. We arrived at Mrs. O'Leary's and I noticed that it was unusually warm for fall weather. After they chitchatted for a good ten minutes, during which I faded into the background, it was time to get to work. What did I have to do you ask? What didn't I have to do? I started by spending plenty of time in her backyard jungle. She had all sorts of bushes, plants, and trees. I swear, a family of hobos could have used her backyard for shelter and no one would be the wiser. My job was to chop up several dead tree stumps into more manageable sized pieces. I never stopped to think about it until now, but chopping through tree stumps with a small axe isn't easy work. My arms were aching by the time I was finished and I just wanted to sit and relax for a bit. No such luck though.

I was then brought into the garage by my father and told to carry all this junk that she was getting rid of to the curb for her. I mindlessly lifted heavy boxes and carried them around for the next who knows how long. I was out of breath and sore by the time I was done with that. Next, I had to tear apart a doghouse. That might sound like fun but let me tell you, that thing put up one hell of a fight. I really hoped we were done after that, but no, the slave labor wasn't quite finished yet. Now we had to go inside this woman's lair. I was dead tired but my dad seemed to still have a bit of stamina left in the tank. We put up a section of sheet rock on her ceiling that took strength and finesse on both our parts.

Finally the last bone-breaking chore of the day came around. We had to do some painting in her house. I was so relieved because this job actually wouldn't be all that bone-breaking. My task was to paint her staircase. I was not to paint the actual step where you place your foot but the section that rose vertically. Well I thought it would be easy enough. To keep from dripping paint on each step I had to place a strip of tape along the border of each one. Well I wasn't proceeding perfectly but I thought I was doing a fairly decent job. I only made a few, what I thought to be, insignificant drips throughout the entire staircase. My father came to survey how I was doing. Apparently he didn't think I was doing all right. When he saw the drops he started yelling at me. "What are you doing? This is no good. You see all the spots you made?" He began bombarding me with further negative attitude. I didn't really know what to say.

"Well it's not that easy," I meekly responded.

"Oh come on. A little kid could do this job. You're just being lazy and sloppy," he continued on. Now I was starting to get mad. I was tired, hot, sweaty, hungry, and uncomfortable. As far as I was concerned he could take this paintbrush and shove it. Who the hell was he to say I was doing a half-assed job? "Here gimme that brush, I'll finish this," he demanded.

"Fine, take it," I coldly responded. I gave it to him and sat down on the floor near the corner.

I knew this was gonna happen. At some point I figured something I did wouldn't be satisfactory to him. He finished and I avoided saying anything to him. By then Mrs. O'Leary came in and my dad started talking to her. I went and started loading things into the truck so I could get away. My day was finally done. We started at noon and it was now a bit past six. On my way back in I saw her handing him the money and thanking him.

She also turned to me and thanked me as well. She said goodbye and we were finally free to go.

"Well I guess you want your money now, huh," he asked as we got in the truck.

"Yeah that would be fine." He took out some bills and proceeded to hand me fifteen dollars. Fifteen dollars? Fifteen dollars!? That was two and a half bucks an hour! I damn near broke myself and that's all I got! I decided to call out my father on this turn of events in an attempt to understand his rationale. My dad then began talking about hard work this, and value of money that, and gratefulness and unselfishness. Shut up, just shut up. I was so pissed off. I had a terrible day, had little to show for it, and didn't want to hear his rhetoric. Enough. I just wanted to go home, go in my room, and be by myself, without having to deal with my family or anyone else.

CHAPTER 6

Sixty-three…hmm that would be a pretty good score if these teachers operated out of a seventy-five point scale. What were they thinking with this hundred-point nonsense? Ah well, just another failure in my life. I'm used to it by now. I proceeded to do what I usually did upon receiving a bad grade – crunch up the paper and toss it into the garbage. The ringing bell signified the end of my disappointments for that particular day in English class.

I decided to stop at my locker to get a few things. Upon looking around the halls I spotted Kate standing near a classroom door. No, she wasn't the absolute best looking but I liked her more for the fact that she was pretty cool. I wouldn't go so far as to say that we had become good friends but I would say fairly good acquaintances. I felt comfortable enough now to approach her without fear, at least when she wasn't in a group of people. I finished my business at the locker and decided to go over to her. "Hey Kate, what's going on?"

"Oh, hi Greg. I was just waiting for a friend. She has a book of mine that I need for this class. She better get here."

"What class is this," I asked.

"Precalc," she uttered in such a way that emphasized her contempt for the class.

"Ah man, don't tell me you have DeBurns."

"Nah, I got Mrs. Phillips." She replied.

"Good. DeBurns is my enemy. That guy is such an a-hole."

"Really," she asked with sarcasm in her voice. "I heard you guys were good friends."

"Tsss," I didn't even respond with an actual word.

It seemed as if the bell would ring soon. "So it looks like your pal ain't gonna show up anytime soon," I told her.

"Yeah, now I'm screwed. I need a book for that class," she said with a slight trace of desperation in her voice. Oh yes, this was a golden opportunity for me that I could not pass up.

"Y'know I have Precalc too. If you want you can use my book."

"Really, are you sure?"

"Yeah, it's no problem, don't worry about it." And with that I quickly went to my locker to get the book for her. All right, this has gotta score me some points with her. I returned and handed it to her and she thanked me before heading into the room.

I turned and slowly started walking down the hall. Most of the kids were already settling into class. I took my time walking about because I didn't feel like going to gym class today. I got a drink at the fountain and started down the stairs, lost in my own thoughts when suddenly someone grabbed me from behind. I turned and was greeted by Daniel's grinning face. "Where you going punk," he laughingly asked while wrestling me into the wall. I responded by slapping him in the gut and when he released his grip, punching him in the arm.

"Y'know one day when I feel someone grab me I'm just gonna smack you in the head before I even turn around."

"Chill man. So what's up?"

"I don't know."

"You wanna hang out somewhere?"

"Yeah, I guess."

So we walked around the school aimlessly, trying to entertain ourselves. We liked to make boisterous comments as we passed the doors of classrooms to try to get a reaction out of people. It was pretty funny when kids in the class heard us. "Hey don't look over here, look over there," Daniel said to some kids that turned their heads to us as we passed a room.

"Class after class of ugly, ugly children," I loudly stated as we passed another door. I didn't notice if anyone looked. We eventually decided to just hang in the auditorium since it was empty and no one would bother us. We stretched out and relaxed. We would probably be here for the rest of the period. I put my feet up on the back of another chair. "So what's goin' on man? How's everything been with you and Tiff?"

"She was a bitch last night," he bluntly stated.

"What happened this time?" I knew Daniel and Tiff had a good relationship but every so often there was drama.

"We were hanging out, I was already there for a while, right. So we were watching a movie and she says that she's starting to feel like crap cause she was getting her period."

"Uh huh."

"So the movie finished and I asked her, do you want me to do anything for you. She was like, no I just need to lay here for a while. So I was getting ready to leave, it was already a little past ten or something, I wanted to go home."

"Yeah."

"So I said bye to her and I'm starting to walk out the door. Then she's like, you're leaving now? I told her that she didn't want me to do anything so I was gonna go home. Then she started getting an attitude. She was like, you don't even care, why aren't you staying, I need you to rub me, and all this stuff like that. And then she started getting mad at me."

"Right. Go on."

"So we were arguing. I was telling her that she didn't tell me she wanted that. She was like, well you should have known anyway, you should have cared enough to stay without anyone telling you. Yo man, I can't read minds. So we were arguing for a while and then I just left."

"So you left on bad terms?"

"Well she called me later and we were fine after that. But she's such a pain in the ass sometimes. She always wants me to do stuff for her and she always expects me to come right when she calls me."

"Yeah she can be a lot to handle sometimes, I guess. But it's not like it's such a huge deal, I don't think. I'm sure it's worth it to have someone like her."

"Easy for you to say that. You don't have to deal with that type of stuff from her. She just stresses me out sometimes."

"Yeah but it's not like it's bad enough to split up with her."

"Yeah that's true. But it's not like the relationship is perfect. Yeah whatever, so what's up with you?"

"Nothin' really."

"So what about that one chick that's been on your radar? You talk to her?"

"Yeah a little bit." Suddenly the bell rung and the rush of people began. We squeezed into the hallway with the rest of the people. Just then Kate came up to me.

"Hey Greg, thanks for the book. You really saved me," she said as she gave me my book back. "Gotta go," she quickly said as she turned away.

"Hmm," Daniel said while studying her. "That's her right?"

"Yeah."

"You want to get with her right? I think you two might work. So do something about it."

"Like what? It's not like I'm really tight with her."

"So then ask her to hang out sometime."

"You think so?" He gave me a look like I was an idiot.

"Yes," he exclaimed while smacking me in the arm. "And if you don't, I'm going to for you. You can ask her if she wants to do something with a few of us so it won't be too awkward and stressful."

"All right, all right, I'll do it." Crap, I was going to have to make a gutsy move in the near future. I could already feel the stress and I knew I was going to have a hard time doing this.

CHAPTER 7

"$5.75 please." Damn these prices for school food were expensive considering how unsatisfying they were. I'd almost rather not buy anything but I don't feel like being hungry all day. I grudgingly paid for my lunch and found my way to my usual table. The rest of the guys were already there waiting for me. Great, there was no chair at the table. Since the lunchroom was so overcrowded, chairs were a hot commodity around here.

"Sorry Greg," explained Johnny, "but some big black dude came by and took a chair. We weren't about to stop him."

"Good job guys, nice to know I can count on you," I sarcastically answered. I then had to go on a five minute expedition to find a chair. I spied a spare one at a table with a few girls. "Afternoon ladies. Can I trouble you for a chair?"

"Yeah you can have this one," one of them replied.

"But you have to bark like a dog," another suddenly added. They started giggling and smiling at each other expecting me to make a fool of myself. I then proceeded to give a pretty good dog impression and they definitely got a kick out of it. They were clearly laughing at me, not with me, but I didn't particularly care; I wasn't embarrassed. After entertaining those broads I was finally able to sit down.

My food began to cool as I took a bite out of my burger. "So what's the good word, people," I asked everyone.

"Hey, check it," announced Johnny, "at the end of the month The Old Folks (Johnny colorfully referred to his parents as "The Old Folks") are gonna be out of town for a little while."

"All right, beer party," shouted Daniel.

"You know it," replied Johnny.

"Sweet," I proclaimed. Being drunk was pretty much the only time I was totally happy with myself. I was much more outgoing and friendly after some drinks. I wasn't afraid of social situations that I may very well have been petrified in if I was sober. "So what else is new," I tossed out.

"Anyone wanna do anything on my birthday," Daniel asked. "I had plans but somebody messed them up," he sarcastically proclaimed while looking at Tiff.

"I told you I have to work all night," she defensively stated.

"Well you should've taken off," Daniel replied.

"I couldn't," she answered.

"That's cause you asked like, just the other day. If you would've asked last week like I told you it probably would've been fine. That's the problem with you; you don't listen." Just then Johnny nudged me in the arm.

"Oooo, trouble in paradise," he said to me with a slight grin.

"Well sorry," she defended, "but I don't have time to sit on my ass all day like you."

"You see what I have to deal with," he only half-jokingly said to Johnny and me. "Sorry, I mean, I only wanted my girlfriend to be with me on my birthday but I guess that's too much to ask."

"All right, I'm sorry, geez. Why do you have to keep on it? Just shut up already," she responded, very annoyed.

"Hey, come here," Daniel said in a warm tone as he went in to grab her.

"Don't touch me," she responded. I could tell now that she wasn't completely serious but she was definitely getting her negative feelings out in a lighthearted way. "You're mean to me. You don't appreciate me. See, Greg here appreciates me," she said as she put her arms around me and rested her head on my shoulder. I put my head against hers and rubbed her arm for a few seconds. After the joke had run its course Daniel jumped in.

"All right, enough. Give her back," he said while pulling us apart. He sarcastically spoke, "I may not want her but I won't let anyone else have her either." He then tilted his head back and gave an over the top evil villain laugh while grabbing her. After that, things seemed to relatively go back to normal with them. Their relationship was kind of strange in the fact that their emotions could quickly change in the heat of the moment. "So yeah, anyways, I don't have anything set for Thursday. Am I going to be celebrating my birthday all alone?"

"I'm sure we can dig up some trouble," I offered.

"Yeah, I'm down. We'll do something cool," Johnny added.

"See, they're not ditching me," he said to her in a mildly spiteful manner. She responded by pushing his face away from her.

"Yo Daniel let me see your phone for a minute," Johnny asked.

"Yeah here man."

"I just got a new cell. I'm gonna put my number into yours," Johnny said while fiddling with Daniel's phone. "Who's J?"

"Huh," Daniel asked.

"There's a contact here that just says, J." Hmm…I thought to myself.

"Oh, that's Justin Miller. I didn't have time to put his whole name in cause we were in class. Y'know that tall kid, he's into metal, he has a few Iron Maiden shirts? He's selling a guitar and I wanna take a look at it."

"Yo that kid is weird," I stated.

"Yeah and he sometimes smells funny," added Johnny while tossing Daniel back his phone.

"Yeah like you don't," Daniel fired back.

"Yo, my stank is an incurable genetic condition," Johnny jokingly said. I smelled the air close to him and said that he smelled like burnt ham fat while pretending to gag. Tiff got a good kick out of that remark and laughed pretty hard.

"Greg, you're so mean," she said.

"Only to the people I hate," I retorted.

"Hey Greg," Daniel shifted the conversation, "ask that girl if she wants to hang out with us sometime."

"You mean that chick Kate," asked Johnny.

"Yeah," I answered.

"Yeah tell her to come to the movies with us sometime," Johnny offered.

"I guess I'll ask her sometime soon," I said in the hope that they wouldn't press the conversation concerning her any further.

"You better," Tiff encouraged. Johnny got up and started getting his stuff together.

"All right guys, I'm out. Anyone coming with me," he asked.

"Yeah I'm coming," I replied. "How 'bout you guys," I asked Daniel and Tiff.

"Nah, we're gonna stay here," Tiff answered.

"Nice to see you making the decisions for both of us," Daniel chimed in.

"All right Greg, let's roll."

"See ya guys," I stated as we left.

On our way up the stairs we saw old man Marshall, the grizzled wood shop teacher. "Hey Marshall you owe me an absence note form," Johnny called to him.

"And you owe me a functioning cabinet, Brewer," he replied back. Ah, touché. Marshall was probably my favorite teacher. You could always

BS with him. "You two hooligans better not be getting into any trouble now," he warmly said to us while passing.

"And you better not be putting too much pressure on that wooden hip or you'll fall down these stairs," I said to him. Me and some guys liked to joke about him constructing his own hip in the shop.

"You guys are too much," he laughingly said while turning down the hall.

While continuing our walk we decided to stop by my locker. When we got to my floor Johnny looked down the hall and began tapping my arm with the back of his hand. "Hey it looks like Kate down there," he said to me. I had a look for myself and confirmed that it was her. As she got closer and saw us she greeted us.

"Hi guys."

"Hey," Johnny replied.

"Hi Kate," I said.

"Yeah," began Johnny, "I was on my way to the bathroom. I'll see you guys. Later Greg," he said as he made his way down the hall. I knew that he had strategically left us alone.

"So how you doin'," I asked.

"Pretty good actually. Today is my birthday."

"Is it really?"

"Yeah."

"Oh wow. Well I hope you have a happy birthday," I wished her.

"Thank you."

"If I knew, maybe I would've got you something."

"Oh no, you wouldn't need to do that."

"Well that's the kind of nice SOB I am," I remarked in an attempt to get her to possibly chuckle. She gave a little smile.

"I have this project I'm doing today. I'm kinda nervous," she began.

"What's it about?"

"You had to pick something that was significant to culture. I did mine on the music of The Beatles."

"The Beatles are cool. I'm sure you'll do great," I said trying to support her.

"I hope so."

"Hey I got a raise at my job," I informed her. "I'm a whole fifty cents over minimum wage. Now I can afford that new car with ease," I jokingly said.

"Well it's better than nothing. At least you're not totally broke."

"Yeah I guess." We talked for another couple of minutes. Hmm, I thought. Now would be a pretty good chance to ask her to hang out.

"All right I have to go," she told me. Yeah I better ask her now.

"Ok," I replied. This is it. I better go for it.

"See ya around," she said as she began to walk. It's now or never.

"Hey Kate," I said as she turned around. I could feel the heaviness in my stomach. "Good luck on your project."…Damn it! I couldn't do it. I had the perfect opportunity and I chickened out.

"Thanks, I appreciate it," she responded.

"Yeah don't mention it," I said cheerfully while thinking to myself dejectedly.

CHAPTER 8

"Good morning heartache, you're like an old friend, come to see me again." Yeah, right on, sing it Tim. I had been laying in my bed for nearly an hour just listening to music. I was partway through one of my Rancid albums. I wasn't in that great of a mood to begin with so I just didn't feel like doing anything. This was a somewhat typical routine of mine – feeling down and listening to songs that were depressive. After that I would usually go to sleep for a few hours. At least when I was asleep I wouldn't have anything to be unhappy about.

I woke up two hours later, not feeling much different. Man, this sucks. I had nothing to do. I figured I'd go outside, get some air or something. I got in my car and just sat in the seat for a minute. Even though I wasn't actively thinking about it, I was still vaguely aware of my failure with Kate last week. Well, no sense in beating myself up over it the whole day. I decided I would just drive around. Just then my mom came home. After she parked in the driveway she saw me and motioned for me to roll down the window. "Where are you going," she asked.

"Nowhere."

"What do you mean nowhere?"

"I don't know."

"Then why are you sitting in your car?"

"I don't know," I replied back, getting increasingly annoyed. Just go away please. "I guess I'm going to some stores or something."

"Will you be back for dinner?"

"No," I yelled conclusively while rolling up my window. I put the car in drive and rolled down the street. I had no particular destination and just drove about aimlessly for a good ten minutes. Yeah, this sucks. I didn't want to go back so I decided to stop by and see if Johnny was home. I was in luck as I pulled up near his house. His dad was outside and told me Johnny just arrived. I entered the Brewer household and made myself comfortable. I grabbed a few snacks and a drink before bursting into his room. "Yo," I proclaimed while plopping down in his chair.

"'Sup man, what's goin' on," he asked.

"I don't know. I didn't feel like being at my house anymore."

"I hear that." After exchanging pleasantries for a bit we then wasted an hour or two watching TV and listening to music, while cracking jokes. "You wanna go down to the Grill Express and get some burgers or somethin'?"

"Yeah, I'm hungry," I complied. We got in Johnny's car and sped towards our destination. That was the way Johnny usually drove – fast. We pulled into the parking lot and managed to slip into one of the very first spaces. We sat down at our usual booth in the back corner while waiting for our waitress. When she arrived I ordered my usual – two chili dogs and fries.

"So what's the status with this chick," Johnny plainly asked. Oh geez. I had been dreading talking about this.

"Umm…I'm still just talking to her. I haven't really made too big of a move yet."

"How long have you been associating with her? A month, a month and a half?"

"Yeah something like that," I answered.

"Well," he started, offering me advice, "I think you should do something about it by now. There's no sense in keeping yourself in suspense forever. That's just going to lead to unnecessary stress."

"You're right," I agreed.

"You gotta ask her to hang with us. How 'bout tomorrow? It's a Friday night. You, me, Daniel, and Tiff can go to a movie. Ask her to come with us. Corner her and ask her at lunch tomorrow."

"Yeah that sounds like a fair plan. Whatever happens, just don't let me chicken out, ok?"

"If you do I'll murder you," he said to me with a stone cold face. So the plan was now set. Tomorrow would be an interesting day indeed. We finished up eating and left, cruising out of the parking lot with the windows down and the radio up. I talked with Johnny a little more before exiting his car and getting into mine.

"See ya man," I told him.

"Yeah take it easy. Tomorrow is your big day, champ."

"Yeah, I know," I said before getting out. I then got in my car and drove home through the night.

I woke up the next morning surprisingly refreshed. Normally I'm dead tired cause I go to sleep so late, but I actually turned in at a decent time last night. I was in the process of getting ready when I couldn't decide what to wear. Hmm…maybe I should wear something nice today. I put on my black jeans and my collared, button up shirt – nice, but not too conformist looking. I looked respectable but still cool, or so at least I thought. Anyway, it was time for some breakfast, or in this case a pack of Pop-Tarts. My parents were in the kitchen. My mom was watching the weather channel while my dad was occupying himself with the newspaper. I ate standing up while my parents talked amongst themselves. Eventually they tried to incorporate me into their conversation. My dad commented on the school's football team. "So you won again last week, huh?"

"Yeah I guess," I answered him. I had pretty much no interest in the football team.

"I think your team can make the playoffs this year. Should be exciting."

"Yeah, should be," I vacantly replied.

"So Greg," my mom jumped in, "I heard the elections for student government are coming up soon."

"Yeah, like next week or something," I confirmed.

"Isn't that interesting," she asked.

"Umm…no, not really. It doesn't matter who gets elected. It's not like anything they do will actually make a difference to anyone." That's the opinion I left them with before finally heading out the door to leave for school. I arrived fifteen minutes before class and spotted Paul, an acquaintance of mine from math class. I asked him if he had done the ditto for homework and he replied that he did.

"Yeah, if you need to copy it here it is but I'm not guaranteeing how right it is," he offered.

"Doesn't matter," I answered back. As long as it gets done. We usually helped each other to get through the class because, after all, doing half the work was much easier. After sitting through math, where surprisingly DeBurns didn't do anything to make me hate him, and a few other classes, it was time for lunch and my moment of truth. I met Johnny and Daniel at the table. "So, you gonna ask her to come with us to the movies tonight," Daniel immediately asked.

"Yeah I will," I assured him.

"Do you want us to be with you when you ask her or do you want to do it alone," asked Johnny.

"I'll ask her myself." I spied her entering the serving area and decided to make my move. The guys wished me luck. I got in there and seeked her out. "Hey Kate," I greeted her. She greeted me back and asked how I was doing. "Fine," I quickly answered. I decided I better cut through the crap and get to the point. I was pretty anxious. "Hey, me and a few friends are going to the movies tonight. Johnny, you met him, and my other friends, Tiffany Warner, you know who she is, and her boyfriend

Daniel." Whew, ok you're doing good. Keep going. "Do you think you'd be interested in coming with us?" Now let me just say that that sounded more confident than I really was. What would her response be? Being a fairly pessimistic person I had, in my mind earlier today, expected the worst. In fact, right now, I was mentally preparing myself for the emotional equivalent of a punch in the face. Surprisingly, the punch didn't connect. However, that isn't to say I was victorious though.

"Oh, I'm sorry, I'm busy tonight. I have to baby-sit for a friend of the family," she informed me. Well that wasn't what I expected to here.

"Oh, are you? Well that's ok," I replied. I didn't want to press her any further so I just left it at that.

"I'll see you Monday," she told me as she paid for her lunch and made her way through the cafeteria. I returned to my table and informed the gang. Tiff had just shown up a few minutes ago. I wasn't sure exactly how I felt.

"Well she didn't say no," Daniel happily told me.

"Yeah that's true. But she also didn't give me any indication as to whether she actually wanted to come or not."

"Well then just ask her again sometime," Tiff advised me.

"Yeah, I guess we'll have to see how this goes," I said while curiously contemplating the uncertainty of the situation.

CHAPTER 9

Me, Daniel, Johnny, and Tiffany were hanging out at her house. It was a few hours later that same day. "So what are we doing tonight," Tiff asked. "Are we still going to the movies? Which one of you wants to check the show times?"

"Not me."

"Ehh."

"No thanks." She just received three negative answers. I guess that meant we dropped the movie idea.

"You guys suck," she emphatically stated. "Well who has any better ideas?"

"We can just stay here," I offered.

"Screw that. I spend enough time living here," she countered.

"Let's go to the mall," Johnny requested.

"Fine with me," I said.

"Yeah, I wanna go shopping for a few things," Tiff excitedly agreed.

"Gee, I wonder who's gonna have to pay for half your crap," said Daniel.

"Quit complaining, I buy you stuff just as often as you do for me," Tiff responded.

"Yeah ok," I saw Daniel silently mouth to me while Tiff wasn't looking.

"Well let's go then kids," stated Johnny while getting up. We proceeded to walk out the door and on my way I grabbed a can of soda. We got into Daniel's car; Tiff took shotgun while me and Johnny got in the back. It was a little tight at first until we cleared some of the junk out of the way. Daniel had all sorts of books, magazines, music tapes and discs, and other various items clogging his backseat. We hit the highway to Elvis' "Jailhouse Rock". Daniel had a pretty wide range of musical taste, which was pretty cool. He got his musical inspiration from a bunch of different places. He played guitar and wasn't half bad. For a few years now it had been a fantasy of ours to form a band and become famous. We had the idea that I would play drums (although I thought I sucked), Daniel would play guitar, and Johnny, who was at least a competent bass player, could sing as well. I don't know why but things never clicked. We never practiced with each other as much as we should have and also, as we learned through much frustration, the business of songwriting was much harder than any of us imagined. We would jam from time to time but it didn't seem like anything significant was actually going to come out of it.

I didn't really say much the entire car ride as my mind kept wandering to other things. I analyzed the Kate situation of earlier today in my mind. I kept trying to come up with any clue as to whether she was interested in hanging with me or not. I couldn't form an answer. I couldn't figure out how she seemed – actually, she did seem busy, that's about all I could gather.

I also thought about how unsatisfying my home life was. I didn't feel particularly close to either of my parents. I especially felt as if I couldn't talk to them about much. They weren't bad people, I just felt distant from them. I thought about my schoolwork. I was passing nearly all my classes but not with any grades to be proud of. I was a mediocre student at best. I still hadn't figured out what college I wanted to go to. I still hadn't figured out if I even wanted to go to college – period. I had no idea what lay ahead for me after graduation.

I thought about my drum set and how it now only represented a lost dream. If only I had stayed dedicated maybe my hope wouldn't have slipped away. I thought about my job and concluded that it was just filler. It was really just a way to collect a small amount of money each week because I would never be able to move through the glass ceiling of our store's structure.

I thought about my unfulfilling social skills. I would never be popular or well known. I wouldn't be the center of attention or have everybody wanting to be my friend. Hell, I didn't even know when I would achieve the romantic companionship I'd been longing for all my life. All these thoughts were swirling around my head and were weighing down on me. We parked the car and it felt good to open the door and get some air. It was a Friday night so the mall was going to be crowded with kids. "I wonder how many good looking honeys are going to be in there looking at me," Johnny exclaimed as we made our way through the parking lot.

"Honeys," questioned Tiffany. "Johnny, why don't you try and meet a nice girl and stick with her for once?"

"I don't know if I wanna be held down. I mean, I don't wanna turn into Daniel here," he said while making whipping motions with his hand. "Woo-chh, woo-chh."

"Hey Johnny, you know what I think about that," Daniel asked.

"What?" Daniel then reared back and punched Johnny in the arm pretty hard. "Oww, ahh, holy crap," Johnny exclaimed while gripping his arm tenderly. We all burst out laughing at this – that is, all except for Johnny. We made our way inside, passing some younger kids who looked like they were trying way too hard to be cool. Once we were in we sifted through the crowd congregating near the doorway.

"Ok, where are we going," I asked.

"I wanna get some clothes," Tiff requested.

"All right, let's go," Daniel said. We entered one of the shops and while Tiff and Daniel were looking around, me and Johnny sat down in some chairs. About twenty minutes later they came back to us.

"So what are you getting," Johnny asked.

"I'm getting this belt, this little bracelet, this sweatshirt, and I'm thinking about a pair of pants. I'm gonna go try them on now." The belt was studded with this cool little star as the buckle. The sweatshirt was just a plain black hoody. She came back out wearing the pants; they were a blue pair of cargoish pants that were cool looking and sexy at the same time because they were slightly tighter than stuff she usually wore. I was a little surprised because Tiff was pretty cautious about how revealing her clothes were. "What do you think Greg," she asked me.

"Well I'll be honest," I replied. "I like them. They're cool and they also make your butt look good."

"Well in that case I think I'll go with them. Thanks doll," she said while stroking my chin.

"No problem princess," I replied.

"Hey lovers break it up," Daniel said while getting in between us.

"So you ready to go yet," I asked him.

"Ask the queen over here," he replied.

"Yeah I'm ready guys. We can leave now, let me just pay for this stuff. Come on Daniel," she said while grabbing his hand.

Next, we headed into the rock and roll memorabilia store. We all liked this store so we spent a while looking. After about forty-five minutes I finally decided on a Sex Pistols shirt I had been eyeing up. The other thing I had been eyeing up was one of the cashiers. She was this little blond girl with a rocker style. She was quite attractive. However, I knew I wasn't going to talk to her. There was no way I could come on to a complete stranger; I would be way too scared. I knew from prior bitter experience that this was one of those people that I could only look at, not actually talk to. After paying for my shirt we left the store. "Hey you should've talked to that girl, Greg," Daniel said.

"Nah," I replied.

"You didn't think she looked good?"

"She was all right but I don't know…" I vaguely and untruthfully trailed off.

"You have to stop being so damn picky man," he said.

"Shut up. I don't care for your advice," I joked to him.

"Your loss man," he informed me. We hit a few more stores before the subject of food came up. "You guys wanna eat at the food court," Daniel asked the group. The answer was a unanimous yes. It was pretty crowded as we all got our food and claimed a table. We had been eating and talking for a good ten minutes when Johnny blurted out, "Hey Greg check it out, Kate's over there."

"Don't screw with him," Tiff defended.

"No I'm serious," he replied. "I'm pretty sure that's her over there at that table with the two other girls." We studied them for a few moments before I concluded it was her.

"What the hell, I thought she said she was busy tonight," I wondered aloud.

"Well maybe her plans changed," Tiff gave her insight.

"Are you going to go over there," Daniel asked me.

"No. What the hell would I say? Man, that bitch lied to me today. I'm gonna see what she says on Monday. Let's go before she sees us," I informed them. On our way to the car the guys were trying to be optimistic about the situation.

"Yeah, maybe her plans changed," Daniel agreed with Tiff's earlier assessment.

"Maybe she finished earlier than expected," Tiff said.

"Maybe she's babysitting tomorrow and just got the days confused when she was talking to you before. Also, keep in mind she doesn't have your phone number so it's not like she could have called you," Johnny suggested.

"Yeah maybe you guys are right," I said while hoping my paranoia wouldn't be proven correct on Monday.

CHAPTER 10

The rest of my weekend was devoted to trying to keep my mind off of Kate. I spent most of my Saturday at work. We were having a big sale all week and this was the last day, so we had to try extra hard to sell some crap. For the first few hours we actually had some decent business but soon after it slowed down. This signified an opportunity to take a lunch break. "Hey Greg," Nancy said while looking through a drawer, "I'm going to order something when I find the menu I'm looking for. How about you?"

"Yeah I'll get something from wherever you decide."

"Aha, here it is," she happily exclaimed. A half hour later we were comfortably eating our meals. "So Greg, have you thought about any colleges yet," she asked.

"Well truthfully, no not really. I don't even know if I want to go to college. Frankly, I suck at school and I have no idea what I want to do so I'm not sure if it's the best option for me at this point." See, the cool thing about Nancy was that even though she was an adult she could relate to you and she was usually pretty supportive.

"Well Greg you might be right. Not everyone needs to go to college. If you're talented enough and you have enough desire, you can make it in this world. If you really want to know, I didn't go to college. I started working in a department store soon after high school and I was pretty good at selling. Eventually I moved on from place to place up the ranks and here I am as manager of Rexmon. I may not be rich but I'm well enough off not to regret anything and, more importantly, I'm happy here."

"Wow, that's real interesting Nancy," I replied. "Thanks for the insight." Her story comforted me a great deal.

"Is there anything you're interested in pursuing," she asked me.

"Actually, I would like to be a successful drummer."

"Well there you go. That's something that if you keep at it who knows how far it will take you."

"You're right," I agreed. "I just need to practice a lot more." We ate for another five minutes before she questioned me again – this time about something else.

"You know you seemed a little preoccupied today. I noticed you seemed a little different when you first came in. Is there anything on your mind?"

"Yeah, it's something about a girl," I informed her. "I don't really want to get into it too much. I'll just say that I hope things end up going my way; I don't want to think about it too much now."

"I understand," she told me, "you don't have to say anymore if you don't want." A few more hours passed and so I was free to leave. "Ok Greg, you can go now. I'll see you on Tuesday."

"All right Nancy, take care. I'll see you." When I got home I watched a movie and promptly fell asleep soon after.

The next day I was milling around the house when I remembered what Nancy said. Yeah, I should play my drums. I went down to the basement where I kept them and decided to give it a shot. To put it bluntly, I sounded pretty crappy. A lot of times I had trouble keeping the beat steady. And the beats I did manage to keep up didn't sound all that impressive to begin with. My reflexes felt unsatisfactory, I couldn't move the sticks as fast as I wanted, nor could I move my legs fast enough for the bass drum. I really couldn't make anything sound smooth enough. After about a half hour I gave up for the day. My problem was that I wasn't good because I didn't practice enough. I didn't practice enough because I didn't like the way I sounded. The logic was quite circular, and thus, hard to overcome.

I went back upstairs to sit in my bed, listen to some music, and contemplate my crappy drumming skills. I was soon interrupted by my phone going off and I fumbled with it for a while before just angrily throwing the covers off my bed so I could answer. "Hello," I asked in a snippy tone.

"Hi Greg, it's Tiffany, did I bother you?"

"No, I'm fine. Sorry if I sounded angry."

"Are you with Daniel or do you know where he is?"

"No," I responded. "Haven't heard from him today, sorry."

"I can't get in touch with him and I really need him to come by. I don't feel good," she told me. "I don't want to annoy you but, do you think...maybe you can come by," she requested.

"Yeah, ok Tiff. I'll be there soon, don't worry."

"Thank you so much," she said before hanging up.

I arrived at Tiff's house ten minutes later. When I got in I heard her inform me that she was in the bathroom. I told her I would wait in her room. She came in five minutes later. "Ughhhh, I feel terrible," she greeted me. "I was pooping and throwing up for a half hour," she painfully informed me.

"Come on, lay down," I told her. She crawled into her bed while I arranged the pillows for her. When she was comfortable I tucked her in beneath the covers.

"Massage my legs a little bit, on the calves please," she asked of me. I rubbed her legs for a few minutes. It seemed to soothe her.

"Do you think you wanna go to sleep soon," I asked her.

"No, not now," she answered. "Can you put in a movie or something, maybe that will distract me for a bit?"

"Sure," I said while going through her collection. After choosing a Simpsons disc I sat down in the chair beside her. She looked so cute and snug all bundled up the way she was. We laughed and talked for a little bit before she apparently regained her appetite.

"Can you get me something to eat please," she requested.

"Yeah, what do you want?"

"There's a little frozen pizza in the door of the freezer that you can put in the oven and, if you could, make me a grilled cheese sandwich. Help yourself to anything you want while you're there."

"Thanks," I said while snagging a frozen burrito. "All right, I'll try the grilled cheese but I'm not guaranteeing it will be good," I told her. I returned with the food and she seemed glad that I actually tried my hand at the sandwich. "How is it," I asked.

"It's fine," she replied. "Could've used more cheese though."

"What am I, a cook?"

"It's ok," she said while smiling. After she ate she turned over on her stomach. "Can you just rub my shoulders and my upper back, pretty please," she said in her whimpering tone.

"Ok, you got me with the pretty please," I responded before complying with her wishes.

"That feels nice, you're such a good friend Greg." During the course of the next half hour I continued my pampering of Tiff while keeping her company by talking to her.

"Do you still feel bad," I asked her.

"I'm better than before," she answered.

"I'm glad to hear that," I told her. "Do you think you're gonna go to school tomorrow?"

"I think so. Actually I'm kinda curious to see what happens with that girl of yours," she said as she lay on her side with her head resting on her hand.

"I just hope she likes me and she wasn't just trying to avoid hanging with me…but I don't know," I confessed.

"She would be stupid not to like you," Tiff spoke. "You're absolutely sweet, and any girl would be lucky to have someone like you."

"Thanks Tiff. You have no idea but that really means a lot to me," I told her.

"I know if I was a girl you were after I would be glad to have you as a boyfriend," she genuinely stated.

"Thank you Tiffany."

"Ok, I think I'm going to go to sleep now. I appreciate everything you did for me. Thank you so much for coming Greg. You're the best, I love you so much," she warmly said.

"I love you too," I said before kissing her on the forehead, wishing her well, and closing her door behind me. "Goodnight Tiffany," I whispered to myself before heading out.

CHAPTER 11

Well Monday morning came and I spent my first twenty minutes of consciousness scrambling to finish a history assignment that I had forgot about. I had to forgo any type of breakfast if I was going to make it to school on time. "Hey Greg, remember I won't be here tonight so you're on your own for dinner," my mom explained.

"Yeah I know," I replied back before heading out. Remembering I couldn't be late to math any more times I quickly got in my car. I managed to run my school route without hitting any red lights, which allowed me to slip into class with about ten seconds to spare.

"Very good Greg, you just got in. I was starting to worry that you would be late," Mr. DeBurns said to me in a slightly mocking tone.

"Oh no, I wouldn't want to miss this class," I said back to him with the same tone. "You stupid jackoff," I whispered while he turned his back. As a change of pace I actually tried paying attention in class today. I even raised my hand a couple times, although I didn't get any questions right.

Later on, in chemistry, I finally got the chance to talk to Kate. I know I tried to keep her off my mind for the weekend but last night I just couldn't help but stress about the whole thing. It took me a long while to fall asleep; I was so restless in bed last night. I got into class early and sat there waiting for her. She walked in a minute or two later and sat down beside me. "Hey," I said while mentally studying her.

"What's up," she replied. I was afraid of coming off as suspicious so I small talked for a little bit before diving into my interrogation.

"So how did that babysitting go," I nonchalantly asked.

"Pretty lame but what do you expect," she asked. I expect you not to lie to me you deceitful snake! I decided to follow up with another question to incriminate her further and make her guilt doubtless in my mind.

"So how long did you have to take care of the little rugrats," I asked with false humor.

"For a while. My whole day was shot." Yeah right you damn liar. There it is, the proof that I needed. Well, my feelings had just been unequivocally crushed…God I was angry. "And this might become more of a regular thing," she added. Yeah, so you have an easy excuse to avoid me and run around with your friends?

"That sucks," I generally stated. I didn't say anything else to her and the class started soon after. I sure as hell couldn't concentrate even if I tried. I couldn't believe how spiteful I felt toward Kate. She thinks she's so damn smart. Look at her, just sitting there without a care in the world. She has no idea what's going on. I spent the entire period angrily thinking to myself and when class ended I left as soon as possible without saying bye to anyone, specifically Kate.

I felt like complete crap about myself so it was with great reluctance that I entered the cafeteria. I didn't want to run into her again. Actually, I spotted this girl Jen who was friends with Kate. I decided to see what she knew. "Hey Jen, come here a second," I said as I gently grabbed her arm.

"Um…ok," she curiously responded. She was probably wondering what I had up my sleeve. She followed me outside and we sat on the bleachers near the edge of the field we used for gym class. "So what's goin' on Greg," she asked.

"Yeah I just wanted to talk to you for a little bit. You're good friends with Kate right?"

"Yeah we're pretty cool," she confirmed.

"Does she ever talk about me?" Jen looked a bit apprehensive as I was speaking. She looked down for the most part. "'Cause I thought she generally liked me so I tried asking her out the other day. Do you know what she really thinks of me?"

"Oh, well um," Jen awkwardly stalled as she was visibly flustered. I jumped right in.

"What do you know," I urged.

"I guess since you're asking I should tell you."

"Yeah," I impatiently said.

"Well to be perfectly honest…I'm sure you think of her much more than she does of you."

"Oh…all right," I slowly replied as this fact sunk in.

"Do you really wanna know everything," she asked with a slight tone of caution in her voice.

"Yeah, I need to," I informed her.

"All right. So you have a crush on her I'm assuming? Well I'm sorry to tell you that Kate doesn't feel the same. Actually…I'm afraid she doesn't care that much about you at all." Wow. I sure hoped Jen wasn't trying to be comforting 'cause if she was she was failing miserably. "Y'know she never really planned on or imagined being your friend. The only reason she became an acquaintance was because you started talking to her first. She didn't want to look unfriendly so she just reluctantly went along with it. Then she told me that you asked her to hang out. She had no intentions of being around you outside of school so she said that she just gave you some BS excuse." So that was that huh? In the back of my mind I suspected something along these lines but the confirmation of it just absolutely killed me. This girl that I thought so highly of didn't think shit of me. This went from being what could've been my highest point in life to actually being just about my lowest. Jen could see how troubled I was now as I just sat there in silence. It was only about five seconds but it felt a lot longer. "I'm really sorry to have told you all that Greg but I thought it would be better if you knew. It would be worse for you to be led on and have your hopes up for a while, y'know?"

"Do you know why she didn't want anything to do with me," I desperately asked. I needed to know what was wrong with me.

"I guess you're just not her type of guy. I mean, you're just different, and she's just not into the way you dress or the people you hang out with. I'm sorry." So I got all the information I needed.

"Well whatever, don't worry about it, it's not a big deal. Ok thanks for coming out here," I said as I began to dismiss her. "I'm just gonna hang around outside for a little while."

"Are you sure? I mean are you ok," she asked sympathetically.

"Yeah I'm fine," I lied.

"Well…ok. Please don't say anything about this." She said goodbye as she turned to walk away. I sat there alone on the bench for quite a while just thinking to myself. My heart was hurting as I absentmindedly finished the school day.

CHAPTER 12

"Hey, please give me another beer…damn it," I politely requested Johnny.

"Ok man, but I think that maybe I think you shouldn't have too much more."

"Ok," I slowly replied. "It's good to know that you're my friend. You're my friend right," I asked as I raised my hand in the air. The clumsy high five confirmed our friendship. A tender moment between two drunk buddies.

Since Johnny's parents were away we were having a small party at his house. It wasn't that big of a thing, there were only a dozen people or so. Of course Daniel and Tiffany were here. There were also some people from school that I was cool with and a few people I didn't know. I spent the night forgetting about my troubles with the help of some beers. For me, drinking definitely had its advantages. Don't get me wrong, I'm no alcoholic, but I've found out that it helps me. It helps me escape my dreary reality. For a couple of hours I can forget about my problems and just have fun. It also helps me feel comfortable and become sociable, especially with people I don't know, which is something I desperately lack while sober. I can't even introduce myself to someone without overanalyzing it in my head and debating whether it went well or not. After some drinks I become very friendly and approachable and, dare I say it, one lovable SOB with no trace of bitterness about me. As pathetic and disturbed as it may sound, I wish the drunk me was my regular self. Anyway, enough jaded introspection for now.

So there I was sitting next to Daniel, who was thoroughly wasted, Tiff who was still pretty sensible, My Mexican buddy Victor, this guy Richard who I only just met, this girl who I didn't know, and Johnny. During my drunken escapade I told my self-deprecating tale about Kate.

Although some time had passed I was still a little upset about it. Well pain becomes a source of humor and entertainment while in this state so I let out my feelings. The responses I got concerning the situation were ridiculous in their disparity.

"Dude she's a bitch, don't even…why would you use your time on her? I mean, it's your time not hers. If you ask me she deserves what she got," Daniel expertly advised while stumbling through his words.

"Um…but she didn't get anything," I pointed out.

"Exactly! Serves that hussy right," Daniel proclaimed and then burst out laughing. Richard, who didn't drink and seemed like a genuine guy, offered this sentiment: "You know if she doesn't like you for exactly who you are, it's better that you don't even associate with her. You shouldn't have to change to be accepted by someone."

"Yeah man, thanks," I told him with appreciation for his concern.

"I heard she's a lesbian," the unknown girl piped in. We all started chuckling at this.

"No man, believe me," Johnny absurdly began, "she's just playing hard to get. She really wants your cock. Trust me." I promptly ignored Johnny's outburst.

"Hey Greg," Victor began, grabbing me by the shoulder, "you can get a better chick, she's not even that great looking. Man you can get a much better honey," he said in his extra exaggerated Mexican voice that he used when he wanted to be funny.

"Damn straight. I am hot stuff," I confidently replied with more booze than confidence.

The conversation shifted and everyone's attention went all over the place in the next few minutes. Tiffany, who was beside me, spoke quietly to me. "I'm real sorry it didn't work out Greg. Are you feeling ok," she asked with concern.

"Kind of, but I just couldn't understand. I thought it was going good. But screw it, nothing ever works out for me."

"Don't say that. You're a good guy and you deserve to be happy," she said as she put her arm around me and sat beside me. "Cheer up…c'mon, cheer up," she playfully said while trying to brighten my mood. We sat leaning on each other for the next few minutes and I actually did become a little happier. Tiffany has a special way of making me feel good about myself that I love her for. After a bit she got up and mingled elsewhere. Now me, Daniel, and the unknown girl were in our own little group.

"So what's your name doll face," I asked her, trying to be entertaining.

"Kristen," came her answer as I reached out, took her hand, and kissed it. Damn, I was out of my mind but I guess she was too cause she didn't get upset. For the next few minutes me and Daniel talked to her and proceeded to bombard her with every memorable story about our friendship that we could think of.

"…So he whipped the tennis ball at the back of my head! Now I'm ready to thrash him within an inch of his twelve year old life," I narrated in the middle of one rambling story.

"Um, yeah. I have to go over there now," she quickly said as she got up to change her seat. I guess she didn't want to listen to us idiots all night.

"Hey sorry about that time man," Daniel slurred his words to me.

"It's all right. After all, you're my best friend," I reassured him as we embraced in a quick, manly hug. "After all, I probably should have apologized to your ankle afterwards," I recounted while chuckling. Ahh, memories!

Sooner or later Tiff came by to get nice and comfortable with Daniel. After a bit I could tell she wanted to leave with him. "Yeah," Daniel said to me and Johnny as he got up to leave, "she probably wants to do it." I never thought about their romantic life unless it was specifically mentioned. For some reason, hearing that made me feel a bit uneasy. I don't know why but maybe it was the careless attitude with which he said it that bothered me. Or…I don't know.

Well, I wandered over to some other guys I knew a little. I wasn't friends with any of these people; I was more like an associate. Apparently they were doing more than drinking beers because one of them handed me a pill of some kind. I wasn't sure what it was. "Yeah man, take one of these. You'll feel so good. Nothing will bother you," he said, trying to persuade me.

"Yeah right man," I said while dropping it into my pocket. After a brief conversation with these guys I decided I was ready to leave. I found Johnny, gave him a good pat on the shoulder, and walked out the door. It was dark and the streets were quiet now. I figured the walk home would be peaceful. I clumsily navigated Johnny's front porch and shambled across the street. After a few blocks I thought to myself, "It's dark, I'm cold, and I'm alone. How fitting." I started to become more agitated as I went on before jamming my hands into my pockets for warmth. I felt the pill and decided to take it out. Hmm? Maybe I should try something new, alter my reality a little, I considered. But did I really want to take a risk on whatever this thing was…I may have been piss drunk but I retained some sense of caution and finally decided I didn't want to make a bad mistake. "Screw this shit," I said aloud as, frustrated, I hurled it into a sewer.

CHAPTER 13

I don't want to spend much more time lamenting about Kate but I just feel I need to state my current status with her. Over the next few weeks I slowly associated with her less and less because just straight up refusing to talk to her one day would seem a bit suspicious. Although I didn't want anything more to do with her I thought the discrete method would be better. By this point I talked to her very little, pretty much only when she said anything to me. Whatever. I was over this by now so I'm just gonna move on.

I had an interesting encounter in gym class just recently. It all started innocently enough during a game of basketball or, as it should be called in our class, "All the talented black and Hispanic kids schooling the awkward white kids". We were losing but I always tried hard anyways because I didn't want to give those guys the satisfaction of completely ripping us. I was going for a rebound along with this Puerto Rican kid on the other team named Jose. We both got our hands in the vicinity of the ball and during the scramble I guess my hand popped him in the nose. It was completely an accident but let's see how well that theory held up, shall we? "Watch yourself man!" Jose warned me.

"Sorry man, it was an accident. I didn't mean that." Hopefully that heartfelt explanation would appease this 175 pounds of Hispanic attitude. Well it looked like he was a little pissed but otherwise fine until someone else had to put his two cents in. Dale, this black guy on the other team, started talking to Jose.

"Hey bro, you gonna let this white boy play you like that? He bitched you and you're just gonna stand there?"

"Nah he just a punk, I don't need to deal with him," Jose replied. Well I didn't want to risk making it any worse so I didn't say anything. Jose got back into the game when Dale instigated some more.

"Yo Jose, this guy just flipped you off when you turned around."

"What!" he questioned.

"No man," I defended myself quite angrily. "Your dick head friend is bullshitting. He's just trying to screw with me."

"You call my boy a dick head?" Oh crap, I immediately regretted saying that as soon as it escaped my lips.

"Well he's talking shit," I said, hoping to appeal to his common sense.

"Yo watch what you say white boy. Talkin' smack like you some kind of big shot."

"Whatever man. It's done, all right," I said hoping to end the situation. Jose just looked at me hard before we got back into the game. I think I heard him mutter something about me being a bitch under his breath but I wasn't completely sure. Well the rest of the game went along uneventfully.

After the class ended we went into the locker room to change back into our regular clothes. I was just standing there, waiting for some people to clear out when I felt someone bash into me with their shoulder. The force was enough to knock me off my feet. As I got up to see what the hell just happened I saw Jose standing where I just was. He said, "Sorry man, it was an accident." I could clearly tell he was being sarcastic, mocking what I said earlier. Some people saw this and I felt like I would look like a complete piece of crap if I didn't do anything. I never felt this kind of emotion before. I never felt this personally enraged. Before I could realize what I was doing I threw myself at this scumbag. My velocity caused us to both lose our balance as we stumbled to the floor. I tried to hold one of his arms down with my hand and hit him with the other but the whole thing was so chaotic. Maybe I got one or two good shots on him. We scrambled for vertical position and he managed to hit me once. I tried to knee him in the chest but it didn't work too well and I lost my advantage over him. He then tried to get his arm around my neck like he wanted to choke me. A few more seconds and he probably could have, but by this point two gym teachers rushed over and pulled us apart. By now we were both cursing each other while being restrained.

Eventually we both wound up taking turns in the vice principal's office. To make a long story short, I got suspended for two days because the fight was stopped before it became too serious and I wasn't the one who started it. Well it's sure gonna suck when my parents find out about this. Instead of going straight home I decided to go get some food with Daniel. We went to The Grill Express and hung out there for a while talking. I informed him about my cheap ass suspension and told him the whole story. "Yeah those thug pieces of trash think they can do whatever they want," he said with disdain in his voice. We spent a while discussing what's wrong with our school before the subject changed.

"Yeah listen to this man," Daniel told me.

"Here we go," I replied.

"Tiff was freakin' crazy last night. You know she was already in a pissy mood because she had a bad day at work, she was fighting with her parents, and she had her period. So by the time I got to be with her she was like a walking stick of dynamite, man. The whole night was like a well-planned trap, except that no one planned it. I was a little late picking her up – strike one. During the night she wanted me to take her to the mall so she could blow the rest of her money on some useless crap. I tried to teach her a little something about responsibility so I refused to take her – strike two. She was being all around miserable so I wanted to leave. Apparently she didn't think I spent enough time with her – strike three. Oh man you better believe strike three."

"So what happened man," I asked him.

"Well I'll cut around all the drama but she basically told me to leave. Man this is messed up cause it's always me trying to leave and her getting pissed when I do. It was weird, she was actually the one who decided I should leave. I didn't know what the hell to think so I left. I figured I'd do what she says so I don't make it any worse."

"Dude, that's some heavy stuff," I concurred. "So what do you think this means?"

"I have no idea. That sounds like a question I should be asking you."

"Umm…man I don't know. It always seemed like she's the one who's more attached in the relationship, y'know?"

"Do you think she might not be as happy with me as she used to be," Daniel curiously asked me.

"I'm not sure; I'll admit it's kinda hard to read her sometimes."

"Yeah, you ain't kiddin'," he exclaimed.

"Let me ask you something. Are you as satisfied with the whole thing as you were when you first started?" He hesitated for a moment, pondering the question.

"Well it would be pretty hard to say yes. I mean, I still love her but the negative stuff is more prevalent in my mind nowadays. I just get stressed and worked up more easily, and I think she does too. I don't think we need to break up but we need to take a step back for a little bit."

"What does that mean?"

"We need to see each other less often and focus a little bit on other things in our lives."

"I don't know how she's gonna react to this but if you think it's best then I support you."

"Yeah well, it's something we gotta do otherwise we'll drive each other nuts."

After a little more discussion it was time to leave. I now remembered I had my own problems to deal with, namely how my parents were going to react to my suspension. Well, time to go and bite the bullet. I then got in my car and headed home.

CHAPTER 14

I pulled up to my house and was glad to see that neither of my parents were home. I quickly went in and headed for my room. They better not be pissed; I had no choice in this situation. It was about 7 o'clock p.m. so I was hoping I could buy myself about two or three more hours of privacy and then go to sleep early. That way I could avoid my parents until the next day. Hey, I never claimed to have much of a spine.

I decided to watch some TV to kill the time, it's not like I had to do my homework for tomorrow…or the day after that. After about a half hour I heard a car door in the driveway. Crud. I heard the opening of the front door followed by the shuffling of feet. Should I pretend I'm asleep? Nah screw it. I hung around in my room for a bit but no one came up. Ok, I guess I'll casually go into the kitchen and see what happens. I went to the refrigerator and noticed my mother milling around. She simply said, "The school called today. We'll talk when your father gets here." And then she went somewhere else. Um, ok. I guess she wants the encounter to be twice as intense. Well I hustled to my room and went to lie down.

About forty minutes later the front door opened again and I knew my father arrived. I gave him about ten minutes before I went down for "The Encounter". When I went in there they were both sitting at the table talking. Before I could make out what they were saying they stopped talking for a second and both just looked at me. It was as awkward as it sounds. My father was the first to speak; "I'm a little surprised Greg, and more than a little disappointed. I know the facts as the school gave them to me but I'm hoping you can give me a better story."

"I just can't understand this," my mother piped in. "You were actually fighting with another boy?"

"It was all his fault," I defended myself.

"Ok let him tell it," my father said, supporting me. I tried to appeal to their common sense as I told my story, trying to make the other guy look as bad as I could in the process. After I retold the incident as positively as I could, I hoped for the least amount of backlash. "Well this is a complicated situation," my dad informed me. Complicated? No, I don't think so. Some guy tried to walk all over me but I wouldn't let him, at least not without some resistance. "On the one hand you were provoked but at the same time you started a fight and got into some serious trouble. You embarrassed yourself and you embarrassed us as well."

"Did you really have to start a fight, Greg," my mother asked. "Do you know how dangerous that could have been? You're lucky nothing happened. And you know you shouldn't be fighting."

"Don't you think you could have done something else, Greg? I mean, even you have to admit that that was an irresponsible decision." And this criticism went on for another ten minutes. I knew my parents wouldn't understand. They're not in touch with what's going on nowadays. I was getting more and more frustrated as they went on, seemingly supporting me less and less.

"Well what the hell was I supposed to do," I burst out. "Was I supposed to just pick myself up off the ground and pretend nothing happened?" My parents were slightly taken aback by my attitude. Well, what did they expect?

"You could have just talked to the other boy or maybe just have left," my mother suggested.

"Yeah ok. That would have gone over real well," I sarcastically stated.

"Hey settle down Greg, ok," my father requested. "You did something stupid and now you have to accept the punishment. I don't know why you have to be so difficult."

"I'm being difficult? I got knocked on my ass and I chose to defend myself and neither of you are even supporting me. Whatever, I don't care," I said as I turned around and marched up the stairs.

"Greg come back," my mother said.

"Hey, don't walk away," I heard my father say, along with some other words attempting to get me to return. It was too late though; I was already locked away in my room. I figured they would give me crap. It seems like most people these days are against me.

CHAPTER 15

I spent the first day of my suspension sleeping 'til noon. When I got up my parents were long gone and I had the house to myself. Sweet. I decided to go play my drums for a while because I knew I had the whole day to myself. Usually my parents tell me to stop after an hour or so because it's too loud. I let loose today and played for a while. I tried my best to play to some Black Sabbath songs and actually exceeded my expectations. I was covered in sweat so I decided to go upstairs. Having been a lonely man all my life I've become something of a pornography connoisseur. After choosing a suitable movie from my computer I decided to take care of business. Fifteen minutes later I was good to go for a shower and then started my day.

I grew tired of being home so I got into Barely Reliable and decided to take a drive. I stopped by Daniel's house and decided to wait for him; school was out and he would be by any minute. Sure enough Daniel came blazing up the street a few minutes later. After parking he came over to my car and got in. "What's up man," he greeted me. We couldn't figure out what to do so we just cruised around aimlessly for a while. We stopped at the park and just walked around. We tried skipping stones in the water but we weren't very successful.

"So how's Tiffany man," I curiously asked.

"Well I told her the other day what I wanted. Y'know, the whole give me space thing?"

"Yeah so what's up," I inquired.

"Well," he began, "I don't think she liked the idea."

"What makes you say that?"

"The fact that she completely flipped out on me," he stated matter-of-factly. "She was fine at first, we were calmly talking back and forth, and then I don't even know why, I don't remember, but she started spazzing out. Dude, she's a basket case."

"How bad was she?"

"She was pissed, sad, and suspicious all at the same time. She was crying and yelling and stuff. She even freakin' accused me of wanting to find someone else. Are you kidding me? I told her if I didn't love her I wouldn't have been with her this long. This is the kind of crap that would make me want to get a new girlfriend."

"Do you really mean that?"

"I don't know man. I mean, I'm sick of always getting crap and always being wrong."

"Maybe you just need to give her time," I advised, as if I knew anything about relationships. "Maybe just stay apart for a little bit and you can both come back with a clear head."

"Yeah I didn't see her yesterday and I'm not going to tonight either."

"Well maybe that's for the best," I said. We then spent another fifteen minutes talking about the situation. Hearing the problems and trying to give some advice made me feel like a counselor or something. I hope when I get in a relationship it goes smoothly.

Well the park had run its course a while ago so I wanted to head out. After dropping Daniel off, I went home. There was the chance that someone might have been there but I didn't care. Luckily the house was still empty. I normally don't like talking with my family to begin with, and with the business of this suspension I was on extra guard to avoid them. I was in and out in about ten minutes, like a master thief. Before I could start my car my phone informed me that I had a text message. It was from Tiffany and it said: "I need to talk to you, come over." Hmm, this should be interesting.

I got to Tiff's house and encountered her stretched out on the couch with her face buried in a pillow. "Hi Tiff, I got your message. Is everything ok with you?"

"Hi Greg. Come here, sit down," she said as she made room for me. "I know how close you are to Daniel and you know what's going on between us."

"I figured that's what this was about."

"I need to know what's happening. Does Daniel still want to be with me," she asked with a little desperation in her voice.

"Tiffany its ok, he still wants to be with you," I said, comforting her.

"Then why is he trying to get away from me," she wanted to know.

"He just needs to, I don't know, reset himself. Its fine Tiff, don't be upset," I told her.

"What if he finds another, better girl now? He's gonna leave me," she stated with conviction.

"I don't think that's going to happen. Relax Tiffany, don't get upset. You're stressing yourself out," I said to her, trying to be as positive as possible. I had to keep this up for a while because Tiffany just wouldn't settle down. The more we talked the more upset she got. She was on the verge of tears by the end of the conversation. I had to assure her that she shouldn't get so down on herself thinking about this. After a while, what seemed like a long while, she was ok. "Thanks Greg. I really appreciate everything you said and all your help. Have a good night," she said as she hugged me goodbye. I looked her in the eyes and said, "Everything's going to be fine, you'll see," as I got going. "You'll see."

CHAPTER 16

"Dude slow down."

"Nah it's fine."

"Dude slow down," I requested Johnny. He was going a little over forty mph in a twenty-five mph zone. We were racing Daniel from school back to Johnny's house. "There's cops around after school, stupid," I said, trying to appeal to his common sense.

"He's not beating me again," Johnny stubbornly claimed. "He has an unfair advantage cause he's closer to his car when the bell rings. I have to cover that ground now."

"All right man, I don't wanna hear it when you get a ticket," I warned. I don't remember how, but we had all recently made a habit out of racing each other home.

"Stay yellow, stay yellow, stay yellow," Johnny begged as we neared one intersection. The light didn't stay yellow and Johnny had to jam on the brakes. "Damn!" We sat at the red light for a minute and I looked at some of the kids who were gathered on the sidewalk. Man, I hated some of those high and mighty jackasses over there who thought they were better than everyone else. But, amid all the scumbags, there were some people there that I would like to get to know; there were some nice and apparently genuine girls there that I would love to get the chance to know. However, the chances of that though were close to nil. Nearly all the popular girls in our school were either preps or athletes; even if they were nice they probably wouldn't associate with me or my friends. The car, pulling me away from them, was a little symbolic. Oh, I was tired of feeling unaccepted.

We pulled up to Johnny's house a few minutes later and Daniel was already there, sitting on his trunk. "Nice driving loser," he greeted Johnny.

"I'm gonna get you sometime," he claimed as we went into the house. After we rummaged for a meal we sat down at the kitchen table. It had been a while since it was just the three men hanging out. Johnny was currently hanging out with this girl Bethany, Tiff was usually around with us, and I had…um, well at least I could say I didn't have a ball and chain around me, yeah that will do. Anyway, we really hadn't had any deep conversation together in a while. The three of us seemed to have been doing our own things lately. One thing we had in common though was a slight apprehension about graduating. None of us were one hundred percent sure what our plans were just yet. On the surface we may appear to be going nowhere fast and not caring much about it, but that wasn't actually true. We just wanted to have a little fun before having to totally grow up. We discussed what possibly lay in the future for each of us.

"We oughta do something cool with our lives," Daniel stated.

"Yeah I don't want to have to work for the man," Johnny added.

"Damn straight," I piped in. "I want to enjoy my job. I don't want the traffic fighting-desk sitting-boss pleasing-nine to five-life." We threw around possibilities of what we could do together. We talked about our half-assed band and agreed that the music scene probably wasn't going to work out. It's an unbelievably difficult process and we weren't up to the challenge. There are so many different aspects you have to deal with. It's ok for a hobby and a good way to entertain ourselves but we decided that, realistically, we're not going to really go anywhere with it.

We also thought about pooling our resources together and getting into the entertainment business. Now that I thought about it we all had a good sense of humor and decent imaginations. Besides, with three people you only have to do one-third the work of a real creative genius. I could imagine the three of us coming up with a movie or an idea for a television show or something. This was another far-fetched, yet more intriguing idea.

We then talked about our most immediate prospects. Johnny's dad was a mildly important business type at the office of a hardware company. Johnny could most likely get a job there if he wanted. Daniel was talking about having a career that didn't require a whole lot of educational preparation, i.e. having to go to college. He even mentioned the slim possibilities of policeman and fireman. Who knew he had the idea to one day become the authority figure? And for me? I would want to go to college but only if I could be comfortable and successful there. I really didn't know if I could achieve that. If not college, I have no idea what I would throw myself into. At least if I went, I could have some more time to figure it out. Geez, growing up is more stressful than it seems.

During the course of our conversation Daniel took a phone call. "Hello…hey how you doing…yeah me too…no…a little bit…I'm with my friends right now…yeah…ok…I'll probably call you later tonight…all right…take care, bye."

"Who was that," Johnny asked.

"You really wanna know," Daniel inquired with a slight air of mystery.

"No, I just flapped my gums for the exercise."

"Well do you remember that time we ate at 'Round the Clock and I was talking to that waitress?"

"No way," Johnny excitedly exclaimed. I had to admit I was pretty surprised and a bit taken aback. "You actually talk to her? Man, she was really hot. That's pretty cool." I, on the other hand, was a bit concerned.

"When did you start talking to her," I asked.

"Two weeks ago or something, I don't know. What…" he asked as he looked at me.

"I didn't say anything."

"We're just friends. There's nothing to worry about," he assured us.

"Does Tiffany know about her," I asked.

"No, not yet. But I'll tell her about Jessica. It's not like I'm keeping a secret or anything. Besides, she's had guy friends before. Remember that guy Jeff I didn't like that she was buddy-buddy with a few months ago. So this is no different," he defended himself.

"Well for your guys' sake I hope it's not a problem," I let him know.

"Well I don't feel it deserves to be made into one," Daniel definitively claimed.

"So what's been going on," Johnny wanted to know.

"I've just been talking to her on the phone," Daniel responded.

"So what's her deal," he asked.

"She's two years older than us and she goes to the community college in town. She's studying accounting so I guess she's probably kinda smart. She works a lot of hours at the diner," he informed us.

"Is she single," Johnny asked.

"Yeah."

"So let me get this straight. She's a waitress – just like Tiffany, she's older, she's hot, she's smart, and she's single. It's like a superior version of Tiffany," he joked.

"Shut up man," Daniel countered, "I know where you're trying to go with this but it's not like that and it's not going to happen."

"She probably likes you," I told him. "So are you going to keep talking to her," I asked.

"Yeah. She's nice, so why can't I? It's not wrong to meet new people and become friends."

"That's true," I said, backing him up. This was going to be quite the curious situation. I could only help but wonder what kind of role this new girl would play in the days to come.

CHAPTER 17

"Ok your total comes to $127.86," I told the man who had just spent a half hour looking at boots before he had decided on a pair. "Here's your change and have a nice day."

"Thank you sir," he politely replied as he walked away. Whew, this was my first chance to sit down in the last hour and a half. I had been helping customers nonstop for that time. These were the kind that asked you a lot of questions and kept you with them while they looked at things for a while. Granted, they were usually polite, but damn, make a decision on your own, people. You don't need me to hold your hand for every purchase.

"Finally, everyone's gone."

"You're telling me," replied Nancy. "I just got off the phone with Phil (he is the owner of the store) and he wants an inventory count on all pants and all thermal wear."

"Ughh," I emphatically responded. I was certainly earning my money today.

"I know," said Nancy, "but it's late so we can get away with doing half and leaving the rest for the morning crew tomorrow. We'll just say we were pretty busy 'til the end tonight."

"Cool," I said, confirming my support for Nancy's idea. She was a real good boss, not a hardass at all. Phil on the other hand was someone to look out for when he occasionally popped in. You couldn't let him see you just standing there; you always had to be doing something, even if no one was in the store. We finished our half of the inventory in about forty-five minutes. We then sat down to catch our breath.

"So what's been going on with you lately, Greg? Been to any parties? Do you have a girlfriend?"

"Not really any parties lately, and no, I don't have a girlfriend," I replied.

"You know," she began, "I've been in the mood lately to just chill out. I know you've said before you've smoked pot. Do you have any connections? I could go for a little bit, it's been a long time." I thought it over for a few moments. There probably wasn't any risk in giving her some if I had any; she was pretty level-headed. On the other hand I just didn't feel like dealing with the hassle. Besides, I hadn't smoked any weed in the last few weeks and I told her so.

"No sorry. I haven't done it in a while."

A few minutes later Daniel came into the store. This wasn't unusual; he sometimes came by before my shift ended if he wanted to hang out. After saying our goodbyes we left and headed for his house. When we got there I exited my car and got into his. We would probably just shoot the breeze for a little bit before he left for Tiffany's house. I was fiddling with the radio when I asked Daniel why his car smelled vaguely like strawberries. He tapped the air freshener that was dangling off his mirror. "I got this from Jessica," he informed me.

"Um…ok," I replied, somewhat confused.

"I hung out with her recently," he told me.

"Really," I asked.

"Well, she needed my help. She called me up a couple days ago and told me she was bringing her car to the mechanic to get something fixed so she asked me if I could meet her there and give her a ride home, so I did. I met her there and, you know the coffee shop that's next door, she asked me if I wanted to go in there before I dropped her off, so we went in and sat down for a little bit. Then I drove her home."

"Does she know you have a girlfriend?"

"Yeah I told her."

"Well what did she say about that," I curiously asked.

"Nothing really," he replied. "She just kinda moved on in the conversation after that. So yeah, then the next day she called me again and asked if I could pick her up and give her a ride to go get her car. So I stopped by her house and went in for a little bit. When I dropped her back off, she put the air freshener on my mirror as a cute little thank you."

"You know," I began, surveying the situation, "there's a good chance this girl probably wants to get together with you."

"Well I can't control that," Daniel defended.

"Does Tiffany know you hung out with this girl?"

"Yeah."

"And…"

"Well she didn't say it blatantly but I can tell she probably thinks Jessica is a bitch. I know there's no way that Tiff would ever become friends with her. But I told her, she's hung out with guys before while we've been together so it's not like this is unfair or spiteful or anything. Jessica is nice and there's nothing to worry about so I told her not to turn this into a problem."

"Was she ok," I wanted to know.

"She didn't flip out on me but she was still against it. She's never gonna be fully accepting of the situation. I mean, c'mon, just because I have a girlfriend, does that mean I'm not allowed to have girl friends?"

"That's true," I said. Well, on the plus side if Daniel starts hanging out with her maybe I could meet this Jessica. From what I remember she was pretty alluring. Might be cool to talk to her or meet some of her friends. Me and Daniel talked for a little longer before he had to get going to Tiffany's. "All right take it easy, have fun, and tell Tiff I've been thinking of her."

"Sure thing man," he said as he fired up the engine.

CHAPTER 18

"Hey I hope you don't have any plans tonight," Daniel's message began. "Wait, I know you don't, this is Greg Madison we're talking about." I was then met with a burst of fake laughter. "No, but seriously, be ready for me to come get you in an hour and then be ready for later. Oh, and look good. All right, take it easy. I'll see you." Click. Okay that was interesting. I wonder what Daniel had up his sleeve. I decided to give him a call back and find out. "Talk," he said as he picked up.

"Yo, what's up," I asked.

"Hey man, check it – I'm going to be seeing Jessica for a little bit tonight." Well isn't that a surprise... Maybe you want to introduce her to me and Johnny sometime? "And I want you to be there. I want you to meet her." Whoa. Okay. I was actually starting to get worried that Daniel was going to keep Jessica for himself and not introduce her to the rest of the guys.

"Yeah that's cool," I said.

"All right, good. I'll pick you up in a little bit."

"Yeah see ya man." As soon as I hung up I felt a slight wave of nervousness wash over me. I hope I make a good impression. This girl was a big deal – I mean, she was really good looking and older. I decided to take a quick shower and put on a new set of clothes. You can't be too hygienic in a situation like this.

Soon after, Daniel came by to get me. After making a quick stop at the bank we hung out at his house. We just hung out in his room playing video games while we talked. "Yeah man I want you to be there tonight and meet this girl. Obviously Tiffany is never going to hang out with Jessica, hell she refuses to even meet her. I understand, I remember I was kind of like that to her when she used to hang out with that Jeff guy. I was hoping that maybe there was the chance that you could get together with Jessica…and then if that happened Tiff wouldn't hate her anymore."

"That's an idea," I said, concurring. However, I was pretty intimidated and decided to let Daniel know about it. "Dude I'm scared," I freely admitted. "I barely have any experience with girls and you want me to start at the top? That's like spending a lifetime looking at the dollar menu and then all of a sudden trying to order a filet mignon. She probably has plenty of experience with guys. Sooner or later she'll see right through me for the loser I am," I desperately explained.

"Well look at it this way. If anything happens that's great. If nothing happens, well it's not like you decided to go out of your way to pursue this in the first place. You wouldn't have really lost anything. It's like a free spin on the roulette wheel," he said.

"Yeah you're right," I replied, "if you put it like that." We put the next hour to good use by continuing to blow each other up in our video game. Eventually Jessica called, as expected. I heard Daniel inform her that he was with a friend but asked her if she still wanted him to come by. She said yes. So now it was set. I started to feel a little anxious as we stood up to get going. I hated, absolutely hated, the fact that I was like this. Instead of being excited to meet someone new, I was nervous. I was so afraid of situations that were out of the ordinary. I felt threatened by the lack of security.

We got in his car and although the winter air was cold, I was still a little hot. We drove for a little bit before we got into the nice section of town. We parked in front of a big house that looked to be an adequate palace for a foreign king. "Dude this house is huge," I marveled.

"Yeah and it's all nice inside too," Daniel let me know. "Let's go," he said as he began walking up the porch to ring the doorbell. Jessica answered the door and let us in. She was wearing a tight pair of jeans with a cute pink babydoll top. Her red hair was up in a bun, which I always liked on girls. She looked really good.

"Hey Daniel," she greeted him.

"Hi Jessica. Hey this is my best friend Greg," he said as he motioned to me.

"Hey, how's it going?"

"Hello. It's nice to see you," she politely responded as we followed her into the living room.

"Sit down guys. You can put the TV on." I sat down on a reclining chair while Daniel took the couch. "Do you want anything to drink or something," she asked as she started toward the kitchen.

"I don't have to give you a tip or anything, right," Daniel asked.

"Only if you want to," she responded. We told her what we wanted and then she came back with our drinks, sitting on the couch next to Daniel.

For the next half hour we sat there talking. Needless to say I felt a little out of my element because I didn't know this girl. Therefore I felt more like an addition to their conversation than anything else. I tried to sneak in points and comments whenever I could so I wouldn't seem too much like a third wheel. Just then Daniel stood up and gave me a quick look before he excused himself to make a phone call, leaving me alone with Jessica. Oh crap here we go. There followed a few seconds of awkward silence that felt more like a few minutes. I decided to throw out anything, so I asked her about life at the diner. Yeah I know, real original and interesting. We then exchanged our experiences about our jobs. After that, we briefly talked about our schools. The conversation may have been a bit bland but at least it wasn't uncomfortably silent, which is what I feared. I decided to change the subject to see how she would react. "So do you have a boyfriend," I asked, knowing full well that she didn't.

"No I don't," she admitted.

"Well…are you looking for one," I asked her, making a move but at the same time keeping it vague enough so that it didn't necessarily look like I was trying to come on to her. I wondered how she would take that question. How would she react?

"Well I don't know," she replied. For a second it seemed as if she was maybe considering me for an option. "I wanna tell you, I do have to admit that…" – that you like me, that you think I'm nice? – "I have a crush on your friend Daniel." Yes, the obvious finally comes out.

"You do know he has a girlfriend right?"

"I know, but I just can't help it," she replied. "I like hanging out with him. I would like to be with him but I know he has a girlfriend. So…what am I gonna do, y'know? Oh well, whatever."

"Do you have anyone else in mind that you would want to get together with," I asked to see what she would say.

"No." A few moments later Daniel came back. Good, now I don't have to deal with anything else. The conversation went back to normal for a few minutes before Daniel announced that we had to leave. We said our goodbyes and then got in the car. I looked over at Daniel for a few seconds. Not that I seriously expected this girl to like me or anything, but me and Daniel weren't all that different. I mean, he had Tiffany, who's a great girl, and this Jessica, who's pretty damn desirable, and what did I have? I don't think I'm jealous but I had to wonder, was he really that much better than me?

"You comin' with me to Tiff's," he asked.

"No I don't feel up to it, just take me home."

CHAPTER 19

I hated milling through this herd of cattle to navigate the cafeteria. Our school was fairly overpopulated because a number of the students are enrolled here illegally. They live in the bordering towns but because they don't want to go to those high schools they scam their way into ours. As I maneuvered between two tables to get to my destination I bumped shoulders with some kid. "Sorry dude," I automatically said; after all this was pretty common in the lunchroom. He didn't even say anything; all he did was give me a dirty look. I think he was a friend of that guy Jose that I had trouble with. Well I gave him a look back and kept on walking. Piece of crap.

I got to my table and sat down beside Johnny, Daniel, Tiff, and Bethany. "What's up people," I greeted them.

"Hey Greg," Tiffany greeted me. I hadn't talked to her much in the past week or so. I hope she's been all right.

"Yo man," Daniel said, "where were you last night?"

"I wasn't anywhere. I was just at home; I didn't really feel like doin' much yesterday," I told him.

"Doggin' my phone call, huh? Well next time you wanna hang you ring me."

"Did anyone else have to go to that assembly today," Johnny piped in.

"I saw it," Tiff said.

"Me too," added Bethany. She was a junior that Johnny had been around with for the past three or four weeks. She played soccer but she really wasn't good friends with the rest of the team. She was kind of quiet sometimes but I had no problem with her.

"It was kind of drab. Wouldn't it have been much better to watch that while high," Johnny suggested. We all laughed, not because this was a random statement but because we had become accustomed to hearing Johnny praise the mind numbing effects of pot. "It could've been much more interesting with a re-write though. What if they made those turkeys eight-foot monsters and they would've kicked the pilgrim's asses? Then Thanksgiving dinner would've turned out a little different, huh?"

"Johnny why do you have to dump on everything," Bethany asked. "It wasn't that bad."

"Yeah cause you like history. I bet you were sitting there taking notes," he countered.

"Hey just cause I have good grades and yours suck…"

"Why don't you go bone up for your SATs or something, poindexter? Anyway, onto more exciting news. I think I'm gonna have another party soon."

"Yeah? Cool," I said. I couldn't wait. I needed to have some fun sometime soon.

"Guys, I need some money for the supplies. Ladies get in free of course," Johnny told us.

"How much this time," Daniel asked.

"Only five bucks from you guys. I'll get the rest from everybody else." Me and Daniel proceeded to cough up some green.

About fifteen minutes later Johnny and Bethany started to leave. I was still working on some ice cream while looking over a study sheet for English. "You coming Tiff," Daniel asked her.

"No I'll catch up with you later," she replied.

"Ok see ya baby," he said while giving her a kiss.

"Bye," she returned and then he left. "So how you been, Greg?"

"Not good, not bad – all right I guess. You?"

"Well…I don't know. I've been a little bothered actually," she started. I felt smart enough to figure out why.

"Is it about that girl Jessica," I predicted.

"Yeah," she confirmed. "I don't like that Daniel spends time with her."

"Well," I began, while thinking what to say. I wanted to stay neutral in this situation. "Is that really fair to say?"

"You don't understand, Greg. It's different now."

"Well if you want you…" – my words were interrupted by the ringing of the bell. After that distraction I finished my thought, "…you can talk to me," I said while we both got up to go our separate ways.

"Thank you," she said as she left.

Later that day I found myself at Johnny's house. Daniel showed up about four beers into the hangout. I was fairly drunk at this point. Johnny returned to the room with a few more cans. "You having any," he asked Daniel.

"No I gotta drive in a few hours." I popped the top on my fifth can in a little over an hour and proceeded to quickly throw down half of it.

"Where you going," I wanted to know.

"I might stop at Jessica's for a little while."

"Yeah, what about Tiffany? What's she doing?"

"I don't know," he replied.

"Well maybe she's sitting home alone. Did you think about that," I asked him in a tone that probably sounded more aggressive than I meant it to be.

"Dude how many beers have you had?"

"He's on his fifth," Johnny said.

"Correction done with five," I said while crushing the can in my hand.

"Maybe you wanna sit down," Daniel suggested. At that point I laid down on the bed. I tried watching the TV while they talked. Then I tried talking while they watched the TV. I thought I felt my phone ringing but I wasn't sure. I tried drinking one more beer but I couldn't finish it. I looked at my friends and said a few things that probably didn't make much sense before deciding to rest my head on a pillow. Before I could realize it I was fast asleep.

CHAPTER 20

"One Taylor ham sandwich, a Coke, and a cheeseburger platter with gravy on the fries please," I politely asked.

"For here or to go," the counterman asked.

"To go." After waiting a few minutes I saw him put in my package fries that had chili on them instead of the gravy I asked for. I was going to tell him to fix my order but then decided against it. I'd dealt with this guy before and I didn't feel like going through the hassle. On a side note, he also looked a little like he was related to The Soup Nazi from Seinfeld. Rather than bring it up I just let it go. Besides, Nancy was waiting for me to bring back our dinners.

"Come back soon," he said.

"Yeah sure," I replied, not sounding like a complete jerk but definitely not sounding genuine either. I hightailed it back to Rexmon's to devour my incorrect meal. "Food's here," I proclaimed as I walked in the door.

"All riiight. Gimme gimme gimme," declared Nancy as we sat down at the desk.

During the course of the conversation she gave me some potentially bad news. "I've been talking to Phil lately and he's been talking about maybe getting rid of some people."

"What," I asked, annoyed.

"Well he's not looking to fire people cause he's mad or anything but he might let some people go to help him save money. Taking a lot of things into consideration – how much money the store is making, how many people are working here, and what times the store is busy – he thinks it will be more profitable to let some of the younger guys go. I'm just giving you a heads up." Ah, Phil Rexmon you cheap bastard.

"Well that sure sucks. I guess I'll keep my eyes open for another job now. Well thanks for telling me Nancy."

"Yeah well if it was up to me you'd be one of the ones I'd keep, but like I said, this is Phil's doing."

"You know maybe the store would make more money if everything wasn't so horribly expensive," I said, giving my oh so professional opinion.

"Yeah but that's Phil for you. He's probably not going to change after ten years."

"Well if it really comes down to it, put in a good word for me," I requested Nancy.

"Sure thing Greg," she said. I always liked Nancy. It would be a little disappointing to have to leave Rexmon's, even if the pay sucked. Oh well, no need to worry about something that's out of my hands.

As I left work I decided to give Tiffany a call and see what was up with her. I hadn't gotten the chance to talk with her lately. I sure hope this Jessica thing wasn't bothering her too much but I would bet otherwise. I dialed her number and Daniel picked up. I had to admit that lately I'd been thinking a little negatively of Daniel. Maybe because I was frustrated with myself, because he was spending time with two girls, maybe because he had the type of thing that I would've loved to have and been satisfied with but he wasn't totally happy, maybe because I thought he was making Tiff feel bad. Maybe I secretly envied his position; maybe I disapproved of it. I don't know. I didn't know what to think but I know it pissed me off to think badly about Daniel for any reason. This was my best friend and if I didn't have him I didn't have anything. "What's up bro," he greeted me enthusiastically.

"Hey man, what are you up to?"

"I'm at Tiff's just hanging around." I heard Tiff in the background.

"Is that Greg? Tell him to come by and pick up our pizza."

"What does the queen want," I asked.

"We ordered a pizza from Joe's. It should be done soon. If you pick it up on the way over you can have some."

"Sounds good. Yeah I'll do it," I told them.

"He said he'll do it," Daniel relayed to her. I heard a squeal of happiness in the background.

I arrived fifteen minutes later munching on a slice of pizza as I entered Tiffany's house. I greeted my friends and set the box down on the coffee table. "I spit on one of the slices. Try to guess which one," I taunted them.

"Is it the same one you had up your butt," Daniel asked while chuckling.

"Well played my friend, well played," I told him. I showed up in time to catch the last forty-five minutes of the movie Home Alone.

"Those Wet Bandits had the right idea. Maybe we should rob houses for a living," Daniel said as he got up. "It would beat real work."

"Yeah but then you have to worry about getting cracked in the head by The South Bend Shovel Slayer. It just wouldn't be worth it," I let him know, putting the kibosh on our criminal careers before they began.

"True," he replied, concurring. "Then he would turn our bodies into mummies," Daniel said while struggling not to laugh. Home Alone was one of our favorite movies growing up. "Well I'm going now baby," he said to Tiff. "Give me a kiss." I got up to take his place on the couch. "What, you want a kiss too, homo?"

"Yo kiss this," I said before punching him in the leg. He chopped me in the chest but I didn't retaliate.

"All right see ya guys," he said as he left.

"Bye," we replied as I got up to throw out the box. "Let's go to my room Greg," Tiff suggested. We went in and she closed the door behind her. She sat on the edge of the bed and I sat in her chair facing her. "I called you last night but I couldn't get in touch with you."

"Oh yeah sorry," I told her. "But I fell asleep."

"I wanted to talk to you about Daniel. And you have to promise to tell me the truth, ok?"

"Yeah I promise," I said to her.

"Does Daniel not like me anymore," she bluntly asked. Wow, this girl goes for the throat immediately.

"No," I replied with conviction. Granted, I know there have been instances where he's been displeased with her but there sure wasn't enough to make me say yes to that question. I know how sensitive Tiff is, so I hoped I wouldn't have to say anything to upset her.

"You've met this Jessica, right?"

"Yeah," I replied.

"Does Daniel like her?"

"Well I mean as a friend, but not anything else."

"Then why does he spend so much time with her. Am I not good enough?" Wow, this was a delicate situation that needed to be handled with care.

"Tiff he likes being with you. I mean, anybody would, you're great to be around," I said, hoping to encourage her. "This girl is nice and I guess it's like when you first meet somebody. You're a little curious about them because you don't really know them that well so you spend a little extra time with them to see what they're about." I hoped that didn't bother her because she was silent for a few moments.

"Is she pretty," she then shakily eked out. Crud. I couldn't very well lie and say no.

"Yeah…she's pretty good looking." Tiff got this disappointed look on her face and didn't say anything. I could tell this whole conversation was difficult for her. She had her face down in her hand. I knew she was self-conscious about her looks. I had to help her. "Tiff, hey Tiff, look," I said, trying to get her attention. She brought her face back up to look at me. "Tiff you are very pretty, ok?" I hope I got through to her.

"Do you really mean it," she asked.

"Of course I do."

"Thank you Greg." We talked for a bit longer. I left her room about twenty minutes later feeling as if I'd done some good.

CHAPTER 21

"Dude, I hope you invited more hot chicks for the party this time," I told Johnny.

"It doesn't matter when you're drunk. You should just get with whoever if they'll have it man," he informed me.

"Maybe that's what you do, but not me. I dunno, all I want is a pretty girl that'll enjoy talking to me. I don't need anything else. I mean, maybe I'm being shallow cause I want her to be attractive, but whatever. So, any good looking girls coming tonight?"

"Well there's more chicks this time, some I've never even talked to before, so it should be good."

"Cool," I said.

"Well I'm gonna go pick up Bethany. Are you idiots staying here or leaving," Johnny asked.

"Dude let's get out of here," I told Daniel.

"Yeah we'll be back tonight, before people start showing up," he said. With that, Daniel and I got up to get going. We got into his car and aimlessly drove around for a bit. We had nowhere to go so we parked in front of Tiffany's house and just hung out until she arrived. "You gonna drink a lot tonight," he asked me.

"Probably a little bit; we'll see," I told him. "You?"

"Hell yeah, you kidding me? With all the stress I've been under the past couple of weeks I should just drink myself into a coma," he cheerfully told me.

"Dude what is the problem," I somewhat snapped at him.

"You know, Tiff is being distant and everything."

"She's being distant? Um…maybe it's because of you," I let him know.

"Whatever. I really don't feel like getting into this now," he said as he leaned back in his seat. "Anyway, we need to find you a girlfriend. Jessica is going to be there, maybe you could talk to her some more."

"Uh, yeah, we'll see," I vacantly replied.

Eventually Tiff came home and we intercepted her before she could go inside. We talked with her in the driveway for a while before she went inside to go get ready. She informed us that she would probably come to the party later because she had a lot of crap to do. We left to pick up some food before returning to Johnny's house. He and Bethany were talking at the kitchen table when we came in. The table wasn't far from the fridge so it didn't take me and Daniel long to break into the beer supply. The leftover pizza box on the shelf was a flimsy line of defense against our greedy hands. I at least wanted to be good and buzzed before anyone else showed up. This way I could be a little more comfortable. While we were working on our cans of Budweiser, Johnny made a brilliant statement: "We should do something really stupid tonight. I sure wanna get piss drunk and I hope I'm not the only one." Daniel responded with an enthusiastic, "Yeahhhh!"

"This won't end well," I sarcastically said. I would probably have to keep my eyes on these two jokers.

About a half hour later people started showing up. Most of the folks who were at Johnny's last time came by. Jessica arrived and when she did I suddenly realized that Tiff would be coming by later as well. Uh oh, this could spell trouble. I hope it stays civil between them. Since Jessica didn't really know anybody she stuck close to Daniel, Johnny, or me the whole time. After observing some drinking games, which I rarely played because I failed to see the point in them, I sat down on the couch to relax. As I scanned the room I observed all the debauchery that was taking place in Johnny's house. A small circle of kids were smoking pot in one corner. A guy and two girls had been in the bathroom for fifteen minutes doing who knows what. Some kids I didn't know where hanging out on Johnny's porch being pretty loud. Hopefully none of the neighbors decided to call the cops or anything – then we'd be screwed, most people were massively drunk and we were all underage.

I only had three beers so I was ok to function. Daniel on the other hand was completely hammered. He was dancing in the living room even though there was no music playing. Jessica sat down beside me; she didn't drink much either. She was so good looking. Hmm, maybe I could try to work some magic on her. "So are you having a good time," I asked her.

"Yeah," she replied. "Your friend Johnny is nice, I like him. And Daniel is so funny."

"Why, cause he's had like ten beers?"

"Hey, you guys talking about me," he asked as he came crashing between us.

"Yeah we were talking about how much we hate you," Jessica giggled.

"That's not true, I know you love me," he said in a singsong voice. He then put his arms around us. "C'mon guys tell me you love me." He then positioned himself to lay down on us with his lower body on my lap and his head resting on Jessica's lap.

"Dude, settle down," I told him.

"I'm not moving until you guys tell me you love me," he demanded. From the corner of my eye I could see Tiffany. She must've just come by. I wonder if she had been watching us.

"Oh ok, I love you," Jessica said humorously.

"Dude, hey dude, Tiffany is here," I said, trying to get his attention. He tried to smoothly compose himself and sat down normally.

"Stay here for a second," I said as I got up to meet Tiff. "Hey Tiff, how are you?"

"Hi Greg," she quickly replied. "What the hell is Daniel doing?" I tried to come to his defense.

"Umm…he's had a lot to drink. He's just being a goof.

"Is that that girl," she asked, coldly.

"Yeah," I replied.

"Cute." Damn, she was pissed. She then walked over to Daniel and stood in front of him without saying anything. When he noticed her he got up to greet her. I saw him then introduce the two girls to each other and then he kind of pulled Tiff into sitting down. I wanted to go back over there to keep my eye on the situation and keep the peace if need be, however I was pulled into the kitchen by Johnny and Bethany. I got roped into talking with them for a good twenty minutes. Me and Bethany chit-chatted about how life was and then about me helping her brother learn to play drums.

Various people had started to leave the party so Johnny got the notion that the remainder of the people should go out to eat dinner. I told him it was a good thought and turned to leave the kitchen to tell people about the new plans. He told me to round up the sober people so that they could drive. When I pulled Tiff aside to try to persuade her that going out might be a little better than staying here, she angrily told me that she really didn't like Jessica, wanted nothing to do with her, and had to endure sitting with her for far too long. "There's no way I'm going if she's going," she told me. "I don't feel like hanging around with Daniel's…new friend."

"I know this sucks for you but she's probably gonna want to come. It's not like we can tell her, hey you can't come, y'know," I said. "Let me just talk to Daniel for a minute ok? I'll try to see what I can do about this shit, all right?" Little did I know just how messed up things would soon get.

CHAPTER 22

I went over to Daniel and immediately grabbed him by the shoulder and pulled him into the kitchen. "Hey man, come here for a second. Yo, Tiffany seems pretty mad, dude. I know Jessica wants to come out with us but I'm pretty sure Tiff isn't going. I think you and her should just leave together and do your own thing.

"What are you talkin' about man? I wanna go out with everyone and have some fun," he replied.

"Yeah I know but just listen. Tiffany is really uncomfortable around Jessica so if she comes with us, Tiff is going to be unhappy," I said, trying to appeal to his common sense.

"C'mon man," he said, ignoring me, "let's just all go out. You're coming right," he said with a dumb grin on his face. He was really drunk so it was hard to get to him.

"Dude you know Jessica is gonna sit next to you and be talkin' to you the whole time, right? How do you think Tiff is gonna feel? And if you decide to go without her she's gonna feel like shit so just think about what you do, ok?" And with that I went outside to wait by my car for whoever would need me to drive them.

I was just sitting on the hood of my car, minding my own business, when I saw Tiffany come storming out of Johnny's house. Daniel was right behind her. They stopped on the porch and from my vantage point I could clearly tell they were arguing. Although I couldn't hear everything they were saying, I could hear when Tiffany was yelling. I sat there kind of not knowing what to do. Should I go over there and try to break it up? No, I knew from previous experience that didn't work. They would just continue as if I weren't there. It pained me to see my best friends like this. "Fine Daniel, go and hang out with that bitch because she clearly means more to you than me," I heard Tiffany yell. C'mon Daniel, I told you not to make things worse. Now I felt a little guilty because things might not have escalated to this level if he didn't get so drunk. I don't know what went on while I was gone but I probably should have kept a better eye on Daniel. On the other hand, he was a big boy; he's capable of making his own decisions. Gee, this looked like it was getting ugly. I could hear Tiffany again. "I don't care, I'm leaving," she yelled as she quickly started down the stairs. I never saw her this mad at Daniel. Her car was way down the block so she went off in that direction. Daniel came my way and although he was nearby he was talking to no one in particular.

"Shit! Ahh screw her," he said aloud as he turned to go back into the house. Again, I didn't know what to do. I considered going in to talk to Daniel and find out what happened. Then I thought about just how emotional Tiffany was and that she was by herself. I decided she probably shouldn't be driving until she calmed down a little so I took off to go find her.

I came upon her sitting in her car, crying. Geez, this was a mess. I tapped on the window to get her attention. She looked at me for a few seconds before rolling it down. "I don't want to talk right now Greg, just leave me alone," she said. Yeah, this was going to be easy.

"Please, just talk to me for a little bit. Or at least let me sit with you until you calm down." She unlocked the door for me but didn't say anything. I got in and sat next to her. She was still crying a little. "Are you ok," I asked her. Yeah, dumb question but I didn't know how else to start going about this.

"Daniel is an asshole," she said while struggling to control her emotions. This was probably the most awkward situation I've ever been in.

"Hey you don't mean that. Do you want to talk about what happened?" Hopefully I could get her to calm down. "You can talk to me. You know I'll try to help you with anything."

"Ok," she said. At least she had stopped crying. After taking some time to compose herself, she went on. "When we were sitting on the couch that whole time he was practically ignoring me. He was talking to a lot of other people and he was definitely paying more attention to that girl than to me. I've been feeling like this ever since he started hanging out with her. What the hell? I don't need to feel second-rate when I'm with my own boyfriend."

"You don't deserve that," I told her.

"Then I told him I was going home and he wouldn't come with me. I guess he thought he would have more fun going out with everyone else than being with me…" I hesitated for a moment.

"Hey listen, I'm not using this for an excuse but keep in mind that he had a lot to drink. He probably didn't mean a lot of whatever he might've said," I informed her. Man I felt really bad for her. "I think you two need to talk to each other about everything, about how you feel and what you need from each other. And definitely not tonight, some other day when both of you are in the right state of mind. I mean, Daniel cares about you, don't think he doesn't. He's very lucky to have you and I don't think he would do anything that truly might make him lose you."

"I just feel so confused and hurt," she painfully told me. We then continued to talk for a long while. She told me all about her feelings, her problems, her fears, and her desires. This was pretty hard to take in but I did my best to try to make her feel better, comfort her, and make her forget about the crap she was currently dealing with. I just sat there looking at her, wondering what Daniel's side to this whole thing was. She then began to tell me how grateful she was that I was here. "Greg it really means so much to me that you came over here to come get me. I honestly didn't think anyone would."

"Well you're my friend and I care about you a lot. I didn't want you to leave so upset."

"You know I really appreciate everything you said. It seems like you're always there for me." As she was saying this she was moving closer to me. "Thank you." After she said that and before I knew what was happening she brought her face close to mine and kissed me on my lips. For a second the warmth of her lips on mine felt good, then my mind started to make sense of what was happening. We both pulled away from each other suddenly but no one said anything. Oh shit. Oh no. Oh shit. What just happened? This was a hell of a situation. She was the first to speak – shakily. "I-I think I need to-I have to leave…right now. Just go Greg, please, I have to leave." I was extremely confused, shocked, and scared. What did this mean?

"Wait, we have to talk right now," I said hoping to get some clarification as to what just happened.

"No Greg, just please let me go, ok?" I didn't want to do the wrong thing but at this point I didn't know what the right or wrong thing was.

"Ok," I said, and no more words were spoken so I got out and she drove away. What did this mean between me and Tiffany? Better yet, what did this mean between me and Daniel?

CHAPTER 23

I walked back over to Johnny's house in a daze. Most of the people had left; only a handful of the partygoers had stayed behind. I ran into my friend Victor but I didn't feel like saying much to him. I asked him if he had seen Daniel and he informed me that he had seen him go off towards Goldstein Park, which was only two blocks away. That was a place me and Daniel hung out to just shoot the shit sometimes. I headed over there thinking I might find him. It was dark, so after fifteen minutes of careful observation I figured the place was empty until I spotted someone sitting by himself on a bench. The familiar army jacket I saw confirmed that it was Daniel.

As I walked over there I figured I had to tell him what happened. What else was I going to do? If he never found out I would always probably feel some degree of remorse about the whole thing, even if it wasn't my fault. It wasn't my fault, right? I went over and greeted him. "If she sent you, I don't wanna talk to her," was the first thing he said.

"Dude what happened," I opened the conversation with. I decided I'd just let him talk without interrupting.

"I don't know, I mean, it seemed ok for a little bit, then she blew up. We were hanging out during the party, she wasn't really talking to anyone or saying much, so I figured if she's being miserable why should I bring myself down? It doesn't mean that I shouldn't have a good time, so I talked to people. I had fun; I'm not going to let her bring me down if she doesn't want to have fun. So then a bunch of people wanted to go eat and I wanted to do that too. I wanted Tiff to come and be with me but she wouldn't. Going out and having a good time was more appealing than going back to her house by ourselves and doing nothing. She never really wants to do anything. It's not like I didn't want her to come; I spent like a half hour trying to convince her. Shit, she doesn't have to be immature about it and cause a scene. She always tries to make me look bad in front of other people. I always do nice shit for her." That was true, I couldn't disagree with him there. "So then she has to have her temper tantrum and storm away like that. I hate that shit. Ughhh," he said as he slapped his hand on the bench. I think at this point he expected me to take his side and offer some sympathy. Or at the very least reinforce some of the points he had just made.

"Hey man let's start walking." We got up and started back towards Johnny's block. "Listen, I have to tell you something. I talked to Tiff a little while ago. This is serious and I don't know how you're going to react," is how I prefaced the following exchange.

"Geez, what the hell happened," he asked.

"Ok just listen man." I then dove into the most unsettling information I ever had to tell my best friend. "After she left I went to talk to her, to calm her down and stuff. She was really upset. So I was in her car and we were talking for a little bit. I was trying to make her feel better, y'know? And…after we were done talking, she told me how thankful she was, y'know, so maybe it was the emotion of the situation or I don't know what but…she kissed me on the lips."

"What," Daniel replied quietly. He seemed shocked and looked like he had a hard time processing the information I just told him.

"I mean, I didn't ask her to – I didn't even expect it."

"So what the hell happened," he asked in a tone that was steadily increasing in its anger. I almost felt like I was being accused of something so I responded defensively.

"First of all, I didn't do anything to bring it on. I mean, she just got close to me and then just kissed me. I don't know what happened." Daniel was shaking his head in disbelief.

"And then what happened?"

"Well we both pulled away pretty quick, then she just told me to leave. She wouldn't say anything so I just got out and she drove away. I don't think she meant it."

"You don't think she meant it," his voice was steadily rising higher. "You don't just kiss somebody for no reason. What the hell did you do?" Now I was starting to get louder.

"I didn't do shit. I was just trying to help her," I emphatically stated.

"Trying to help her? What's that supposed to mean? You don't just kiss somebody out of the blue for no damn reason! She's my girlfriend! Man, what the fuck is your problem!?" he shouted. That hurt really bad. I had never seen Daniel this mad and emotional, let alone at me. Man, what the fuck is your problem? That phrase echoed throughout my head over and over. And it stung more than anything else I had ever experienced in my life. I didn't know how to respond, so I didn't.

Daniel, overcome with emotion, and still fairly intoxicated, turned and started walking in a different direction. I had just alienated my two best friends in the same night. What the fuck was my problem? I was stunned for a few moments but managed to call out, "Daniel! Hey Daniel!" He did slow down a little bit but he didn't turn around, and he never stopped walking. Or at least he didn't stop until long after I lost sight of him.

CHAPTER 24

It had been two days since the whole ugly incident and I hadn't had any contact with Tiffany or Daniel. I assumed they would need some time to figure themselves out, so I figured I would wait for either of them to talk to me when they were ready. In the meantime I was having a hell of a time wallowing in pity, self-doubt, and just all around misery. Well it was just about time for me to leave for work so I got into Barely Reliable and headed out. I usually felt somewhat at peace when I was riding down the road by myself. However, I couldn't help feeling uneasy about what was going on with my friends. I was listening to the radio and Alice Cooper's "Eighteen" came on next. It was a damn good summary of how I felt right about now.

I was cruising down the road, not really concerned about anything, until a police car behind me made its presence known. Now, surprisingly, this was the first time I'd been pulled over and thus felt somewhat apprehensive and quite a bit annoyed. I couldn't consciously think of anything I'd done wrong so I figured I could've been speeding. I sat behind the wheel while the cop was parked behind me. He sure was taking his time. Sometimes when you're in a curious situation strange thoughts cross your mind. For a second I wondered how far I could get if I just decided to gas it now.

The long arm of the law strolled over to my window and very simply, matter-of-factly, said, "License and registration." Um…ok. That was pretty direct. He then left for a while to do whatever legal crap he had to do while I sat there like an idiot. He finally came back after what seemed like ages. "Do you know why I pulled you over?"

"Speeding, I guess?"

"That's right. Are you aware of the limit on this road?"

"Is it twenty-five?"

"Yeah. I had you going thirty-four miles an hour." Without pause he then proceeded to hand me a ticket. A ticket? What the hell? Now granted, I'm no officer of the law and didn't really have any experience with these types of situations but nine miles an hour over the limit? I mean, getting a ticket instead of a warning seemed a little much. It certainly didn't feel excessive when I was driving. He said a few more things before he left and soon after I verbally expressed my displeasure. "Gee, thanks a lot asshole." I expressed my displeasure a bit too soon and a bit too loudly apparently, because John Law heard me. He came back over to me and stooped down so his face was level with mine.

"You know, you high school punks really piss me off. You think you're so damn hot and you don't have any respect." Geez, I must have really struck a nerve with this guy. "Look here you little shit. Now, I can really make things difficult for you. It would take barely any effort to get the other boys in this town to watch you like a hawk any time you're in public. Do you really want that? For now you're not worth the effort though. Now, I'm not gonna ask you to apologize but I'm gonna tell you to just remember that kid. Now get going." Shit, that was pretty intense. I didn't say anything in the face of that raging diatribe, as I was too shocked. However, after getting out of there I just felt like some spineless scumbag.

I pulled into the Rexmon parking lot a few minutes late. Well, time to go work for the man now. I walked in the door and greeted Nancy. "Hey Greg," she replied. "Bad news – I talked to Phil for a while the other day. I'll cut to it. He's going to let you and Jody go."

"Are you serious?" I asked, annoyed but not shocked. After all, Nancy did warn me a few weeks ago.

"Yeah I'm sorry. I tried to save your job but he wasn't having it."

"Well that sure sucks," I said, accepting the news.

"Yeah that's definitely not cool," Nancy agreed. "You have two more weeks though."

"Screw that. If Phil wants to let me go and save money on his precious payroll, than I'm leaving after today. I'm not gonna work and even try to do a good job if I know I'm just going to get fired anyway."

"Well I'm gonna miss you Greg. Why don't you stop in sometimes though? I'd like to still keep in touch. Hey, I'll still give you a discount."

"That's cool. Thanks Nancy."

We talked for a while that day and when it was over it was time to say goodbye. I stepped outside into the dark night sky and walked to my car. On the way to it I passed Phil's delivery van and decided to hock a loogie on it. Not the most mature thing to do but I felt justified. Instead of going home I changed my mind and decided to eat alone at the diner across the street. It would give me some time to think about things.

After I finished my meal I got in my car and drove home. I had nowhere else to go. I couldn't shake the feeling of being pretty useless. Right now I didn't really have anything. No friends…no girl…no job…hell, no life. Terrific, just terrific. I needed to do something to forget about everything else. It was probably at this point that I decided I would start drinking more. A lot more.

CHAPTER 25

I'd been having trouble falling asleep lately and tonight was no different. I turned over and focused in on the red blur that was the alarm clock. It told me that it was 3:56 a.m. I didn't even feel close to tired. All I could do was toss and turn, think and wonder, and try to just let everything go so I could fall asleep. But it was no use. Life sucked and I was sick of it.

I proceeded to get up and do what I'd done for more than half of my nights over the past week. I stepped outside the door and quietly made my way down the hall. I got to the stairs and crept down them slowly – one by one, all the way down to the basement. I made my way around the couch and to the corner where the small bar was. I went around it and examined the contents. Over a dozen bottles of various shapes and sizes stared back at me. My parents hadn't really touched anything back here for a long time. I was free to take whatever I wanted, pretty much without fear. I needed something to help me relax and pick up my spirits.

I reached for the bottle of rum and went to get a cup. Rum tasted a little rough straight up so I grabbed a Coke out of the refrigerator. I poured what looked to be about four shots worth into the cup and filled the rest up with the soda. I discretely put the bottle back on the shelf and took my drink with me. The sneaking around process started again as I slowly and carefully slinked my way upstairs.

Upon entering my room I closed and locked the door behind me. I always did that; it was standard practice – even at four in the morning. You never want anyone else to know what you're up to – ever. I love the feeling of knowing you have complete and utter privacy. I sat on my bed and put on my headphones while zoning out and trying not to think of anything in particular.

My rum concoction was terribly potent. It sure tasted like crap because it was so overpowering. However, I forced myself to swallow it in big gulps. It's like removing a really sticky band-aid. Slowly peeling it will hurt like hell – ripping it off will still be ever so painful, but it is much quicker. I took the same theory with drinks.

After my cup was halfway empty I started to feel it a bit. I lay back on my bed enjoying the different feeling. It was warm and comforting. After a little while, the rest of my drink was gone and I tossed the cup into the garbage. I drank moderately quickly so I was feeling a little dizzy but otherwise good. I felt happy to disconnect from reality. I remembered happier times – when we were all younger.

Everybody was almost the same. No one was really better than anyone else. There weren't really any cliques. People weren't light years ahead in popularity yet and there wasn't too much to set you apart from everybody else. You could hang out with whoever you wanted and it wouldn't seem odd. Man, I miss those days.

There was nothing to really make you feel like shit. Nobody really had any grand plans for what they were going to do in life. Everyone enjoyed simpler things. But eventually people get older and they want more out of life. They were no longer content to hang around and do immature kid stuff that everyone once thought was cool. It's unavoidable really, but still sad. Now things would be different. And you would have to listen to their stories, whether you were in a classroom, hanging around in the parking lot, or wherever. Stories about how far they had gotten with a certain girl, how crazy a certain party had been, how much fun a certain trip over spring break was, and how successful they planned on being in a certain career. And you would have to grin and nod your head, all the while wondering what the hell was wrong with yourself for not experiencing the same things. For not being as good as everyone else.

I looked at the clock and realized I had to wake up for school in another three hours. I wasn't worried about it though. I was a trooper and knew I'd be able to wake up and handle the day on three hours of sleep. I didn't sweat it. I turned over and pulled the covers up to my neck. I was finally comfortable. I fell asleep with a slight smile on my face as I remembered happier times.

CHAPTER 26

It was another typical morning before school, which meant that both of my parents were roaming around the house and I might have to talk to them. Sometimes I just discreetly leave from my room, but if I wanted to eat anything more elaborate than something I could carry in my hand to the car, I would have to endure their presence. Well, hunger won out over sensibility this time so I sat down at the table.

My mom was hanging around in the kitchen while I heated up my breakfast burrito in the microwave. "So Greg, where are you going to work now," she asked.

"I don't know," I vaguely replied.

"Well I can bring you some applications on my way home today."

"No that's ok."

"Maybe the supermarket," she went on, somewhat ignoring what I said. "Or the pizzeria on Wilson Street. Actually, Danielle's Flowers is hiring. I think they pay pretty good." Work in a flower shop? Yeah ok.

"Mom, I'll find something myself ok?"

"Hey I'm just trying to make it easier for you," she retorted. "But you are looking, right?"

"Yeah right, sure," I said, although I really hadn't been. Finding a new job hadn't been in the top rankings of my list of priorities lately. My mom then left the kitchen for a few moments. I sat there and continued to eat my breakfast in peace. I zoned out for a little bit before I got up to get going. On my way out I asked my mom if she was making anything to eat tonight.

"Well are you going to be home," she inquired.

"I guess."

"You haven't been out much lately," she surmised.

"So," I quickly responded.

"Well I was just wondering. Say, I haven't seen or heard much from Daniel lately."

"Yeah, and…" I replied.

"Well you're always hanging around with him. Has he been busy or something?" In a manner of speaking I guess you could say that.

"Yeah, he's been busy," I said as I made my way out the door.

"Doing what," she continued.

"I don't know," I answered as I opened my car door and got in. I gave a wave as I backed out of the driveway.

Twenty-seven minutes later I found myself sitting in the parking lot at school listening to a Megadeth album and drinking a Snapple that contained both Snapple and vodka. There was still plenty of time to kill before school started. Usually people hung out in each other's cars before class but lately I'd been minding my own business. I was bobbing my head along to the music when my concentration was broken by the sound of someone tapping on my window. It was Jen, the girl I had talked to back when I had a crush on Kate. I wasn't best friends with her but we talked a little bit. "Hey Greg."

"What's up lady," I asked her.

"Did you do the English assignment," she asked.

"No, sorry. If I have time I'll do it later. So what are you up to?"

"I don't know. Nothin' really. You want me to sit with you for a little bit. You look lonely all sitting by yourself listening to that god-awful noise," she chuckled.

"What? How dare you madam? Megadeth are great…but I guess I could see to letting you in after a vicious insult like that cause that's how nice I am." She hopped in. "So how ya been," I asked her.

"Great," she excitedly replied. "My dad told me yesterday that if I finish the year with an A average that he would finally let me have my own car. And something that I can pick out, not some piece of junk."

"Like this thing?"

"Hey at least you get to drive, it sucks always riding with other people." I liked talking to Jen. Since I was fairly buzzed I decided to toss out an idea to her.

"Say, you need a ride home today?"

"Well I usually go with Kate and we hang out a little after school. You can come though, I mean if you want." I thought it over for a few moments. I could go and just focus most of my attention on Jen. But I still was kind of disturbed by the whole Kate thing. I decided to take a pass.

"Maybe another day," I told her. "I have something to do today," I lied.

We talked for a little while before it was time to go inside the school. She opened her door but before she stepped out she asked for a sip of my drink. "I don't think you wanna drink this, I mean, you don't know where my mouth's been."

"What, do you have cooties," she asked. I didn't think she'd make a big deal about it so I told her there was alcohol in there. She actually started laughing. "What? Why the hell are you drinking in the morning before school," she asked, incredulously.

"Well," I said, giving her a goofy smile, "the days are long." With that she said she'd see me later and went inside. I got out and headed up to class. I decided I needed some kicks as I got into DeBurns' class. He acknowledged me as I walked into the room.

"Madison," he said while I walked by.

"DeBurns," I returned. I also added, "I must say I like the shirt," while motioning to him. He smiled and nodded in my direction. Without missing a beat, as soon as my back was towards him, I rolled my eyes and made a sarcastic face for all the class to see. A lot of the people near me started laughing and that made me feel pretty damn good. I figured I should start playing the wise guy bit a lot more in this class. It wasn't uncommon for DeBurns to get on my case anyway. If I could entertain the rest of the class on a consistent basis it might help my social standing in this dump. Hell, with a little alcohol in me I wasn't afraid to potentially embarrass myself.

Later on in the day I was talking to Johnny in history class. "Hey man, have you talked much to Daniel or Tiffany since your party," I asked him.

"No man, not really. And where the hell have they been for lunch lately? Either they're not there or I've seen one of them only passing through once in a while. What's up with them?"

"I don't know. I haven't talked to either of them. They had this big ass fight." I didn't elaborate on why though. "I figure they'll be around once they come to an agreement or something, I don't know."

"Well in the meantime you oughta hang with me and Bethany more."

"Hey you two have been together for a little while now huh?"

"Yeah well she's kinda cool." I had kept my drink with me all day and had rationed it wisely so at this point I still had the remnant of a buzz leftover. I thus decided to rag on Johnny for his seeming fondness towards this girl.

"Is my friend Johnny Brewer actually, gasp, dare I say it…in love?"

"No," he quickly replied. I went on, ignoring him.

"Whatever happened to that old, I don't want to get tied down, man's man, attitude of yours?"

"Well we're not officially boyfriend and girlfriend," he informed me.

"Oh but why? You two make an adorable little couple. You should walk around with shirts that say his and hers, don't you think?"

"Shut up loser," he demanded. "Now I don't know about you but I'm trying to pay attention to the intricacies of the Treaty of Versailles. Leave me alone," he sarcastically stated.

"All right, I'll be nice," I apologized.

"Greg, you wanna keep your head this way," Mrs. Cooper gently stated to get my attention.

"Sorry Mrs. C," I replied. I actually liked her and she was nice so I typically tried to be a good kid in her class. I shut up for the remaining fifteen minutes.

After school had ended I found this kid Roger that I was pretty casual with. Among some other things, he was a pretty big pothead. I'd really had the urge to smoke myself silly lately so I figured he'd be a good source. "Yeah man follow me to my house, I got some stuff," he let me know. With that I made the ten minute ride and went with him up to his room. "Yeah man," he started as he pulled a bag of marijuana from his dresser drawer, "this shit is a little stronger than the regular stuff I usually have."

"That's fine with me man," I informed him. We made our deal, which hurt my wallet, but it was worth it. I thanked him and he told me to keep in touch if I needed anything from him. I walked out the door with my merchandise discreetly tucked in my pocket and drove off.

CHAPTER 27

My life lately had turned into a whirlwind of booze and pot. I hadn't heard from my friends in nearly three weeks. I was beginning to accept the fact that maybe they didn't want to know me anymore because of what I'd done. But I didn't do anything, or did I? Maybe in my being so caring and concerned for Tiffany I had accidentally given her the wrong message. Maybe in her grief and emotion she thought that I was trying to be there for her in ways that went beyond friendship. Ways that Daniel had previously been there for her but for whatever reason, no longer was. Did I indeed bring this all on? Was I deserving of Daniel's anger?

No, I was just being a compassionate, sensitive guy. That's the type of person I am, so why couldn't they see it? And for that matter, how come no girls had ever gotten close enough to me to see just how good I was? If someone had, then I wouldn't even be in that bullshit position for Tiff to think I was trying to come on to her, if that's what she actually thought. I was so confused. No, now I was beyond confused; I was fed up, fed up with my stinking, loser life.

The only solace I had now, the only joy I could gain, came from drinking and getting high. Now I was getting drunk and/or stoned every day. I could clearly see that if I kept going this way I was going to become more helpless. I was on the doorstep of turning into something I always believed I was strong enough to never be – an addict. The funny thing was I really didn't care. The past few weeks had fully exposed my, I have nothing to lose, attitude.

As was what had regularly become the case after school ended, I didn't have much to do. I decided to take a ride to my former place of employment and see what was shaking. As I pulled into the parking lot I spotted Phil's delivery van. What that meant was that some higher-up, or perhaps even Phil himself, was here, handling some business inside the store. I didn't feel like enduring the attention or the awkwardness that would surely transpire if I went in and encountered someone I knew. I decided to wait in the parking lot until whoever it was that had stopped by came out. So I bided my time sitting in the car like some sort of outcast. Whenever someone came by with a delivery they were usually gone in a short while. All they really had to do was unload the truck and go over the checklist of merchandise. Sometimes they might stay and chat for a few minutes but their stays were usually short.

I'd been patiently waiting for about ten minutes before I had the opportunity to see who was here. Then I saw him walk by the front window – it was Phil. Ha, the big man himself was actually here; what were the odds? I decided that when he walked out I would be on my way walking in. Let's see just how he would greet me, if he acknowledged me at all. I saw him in there talking to Nancy for a few moments before he started heading for the door. I made my move and got out of the car, determined to explore the curiosity that awaited. As we approached each other I maintained my gaze in his direction. I wasn't going to break and say hello to this man. If he had anything to say, let him greet me.

As we came closer he recognized me. "Greg Madison, hi, how are you?"

"Hey," I cautiously stated.

"Listen Greg, I'm sorry we had to let you go."

"Right." I wasn't going to offer him any more of my tolerance than was necessary.

"But it was for the best interest of the company. I have to make sure the store is turning a profit. It was for business purposes, you understand, right?"

"Sure, I understand," I stated with a mix of sarcasm and contempt. With that I began walking past him towards the door. "It's all right, I didn't like working much for you anyway," I said without stopping or turning to look back. If he said anything I didn't hear him because I had already entered the store.

"Hey it's Greg," Nancy called out when she spotted me. She was on the register so I went over to her desk. This guy by the name of Chuck who I worked with quite a few times came over to me. He was a few years older and in college so maybe that's why he didn't get the axe.

"Hey dude, what's up," he greeted me.

"Hey man," I replied. "Just came by to visit the old sweatshop."

"Ha, right on man."

"How you holdin' up here," I asked him.

"Well the money they give you here is just as green as anywhere else so what are you gonna do? Besides, at least I can get a lot of hours here."

"Yup," I concurred, nodding my head. Nancy then came over and asked how I was doing. "Well I'm still alive so how good can I be?" Chuck laughed.

"You have a strange sense of humor Greg," Nancy said before adding, "I guess that's why I always liked you. Did you see Phil out there?"

"Yeah but I didn't say much to him." I reminisced with my old co-workers for quite some time before I decided to head out. I was looking at one of the display cases for a while before Nancy asked me if I wanted anything. "Yeah, that flask there is pretty damn cool looking. I think I'll get it." She chuckled before opening the case and reaching in.

"Yeah it is kinda cool to have, I guess. I mean, you can't not look like a badass drinking from a flask for god sakes. Tell you what, I'll give you thirty percent off."

"Sweet. Thanks a lot Nancy."

"No prob'. I'll take care of you," she said while ringing me up. I took the bag and said bye to my old associates. They told me to take care and wished me luck in finding a new job or whatever else I decided to do. I got into Barely Reliable and fired her up – scratch that, attempted to fire her up. C'mon baby, don't let me down. After three more attempts I finally got into motion. Thanks girl, I think I'll head for home now.

I walked up the porch and decided to sit outside for a while. I grabbed the mail and had a seat. What have we here? Bill, insurance advertisement, letter for mom, crap from school, catalog, another junk advertisement from…a psychiatrist's practice? Yeah that piece of mail should have my name on it cause that's just what I needed. Sitting and watching the neighborhood soon proved uneventful so I decided to call up Johnny and ask him something. He picked up after a bunch of rings. "Yo dude, what's up," he answered.

"Nothing much." I decided to get right into it. "Hey man, I got a nice amount of weed. You wanna do that crap sometime?"

"Hell yeah. Maybe sometime this week or something, I don't know," he answered.

"Cool," I let him know. "What about Bethany?"

"No, she doesn't do that crap. She doesn't like it."

"And she's going out with you? Does anyone else see the irony here?"

"I'm irresistible, what can I say," he smugly stated.

"Nice. Hey I gotta go but give me a call when you wanna smoke that stuff," I let him know.

"Can do brother. Ok take it easy."

"Peace." Good. I felt more comfortable having someone to do my debauchery with rather than being by myself. I felt less seedy that way and besides, it was more enjoyable.

By the time nightfall came I was stowed away in my room with my newly acquired flask (which was getting its first use), my drumsticks, and nothing but imagination. I was banging away on the edge of my desk pretending I was on stage. This is how it should have been, I envisioned in my dazed state. I could nearly see the people shouting and cheering while I beat away on an intricate solo. Man, how sweet would it have been to be known in school as that badass drummer? The attention, the babes, the glory. Damn that would've been the life. I was actually starting to believe it was possible due to the amount of alcohol I had ingested. Yeah what's stopping me? I oughta go downstairs right now and lay down some soon to be classic beats.

That's what I thought as I exited my room but it never really worked out that way. In my disheveled state I remember not being able to coherently navigate myself to the best of my abilities. I remember the simple miscalculation of missing a single step. I remember the panic as so many things went on in my head during that two-second span. I also remember the black railing speeding towards me. But most of all I remember the blood. You couldn't forget it even if you wanted to, Greg. It was all over the place. Flowing from my head. It stained my arm, my shirt, the steps, the floor. It was a crimson reminder of just where my life had gone.

CHAPTER 28

Eight stitches in my skull later and I was back to full health. To say my parents were horrified when I came upon them would be an understatement. The chilling look of fear on my mother's face was a hell of a sight and the stunned look of confusion my father showed was quite memorable. It was a pretty chaotic situation, so in the frenzy I told them I tripped on the staircase and that was sufficient. There were no follow up questions. It was pretty strange waiting for the ambulance. I didn't feel nervous or anything, just slightly idiotic. I mean, I could have avoided the mess if I had just kept my head down, watched my feet, and carefully guided myself down the stairs. Too late though, what's done is done.

After a visit to the hospital and some doctor's magic, I rode home with my parents. My mom could only talk about how scared she was, what an ordeal it had been, and all the drama surrounding what happened. My dad was fairly composed on the other hand. "So what exactly happened Greg," he calmly asked while driving. I didn't think it would be too hard to defuse the situation.

"I was just going down the stairs and I stumbled. I tried to regain my balance or stop myself but I just couldn't. So I fell and my head hit the railing." There, that should cover all my bases, heh, heh, heh.

"Gee, that was just a random freak accident. But you're lucky it wasn't worse."

"Worse? It was pretty bad," I pointed out.

"True, but you could have easily hit your head again when you landed on the floor," he informed me. Hmm, I hadn't thought about that. Yeah, cracking my head on the tile floor as well would have greatly sucked, to put it bluntly.

"Well accidents happen," I told them, satisfied with the knowledge that they apparently believed this to be an unfortunate accident. I sure didn't want to deal with their reactions to finding out that I'd been drinking all the time, let alone that being the reason why I busted my head in the first place. Yup, I think it would be best to keep my damn fool mouth shut in regards to that little detail.

When I got home the first thing I did was go into the bathroom and check my head for damage. I wondered if there would be some sick scar or something. Well, I really couldn't see the results unless I moved my hair out of the way so no one else was going to see it if they were just walking by. I looked at the mirror and stopped to think for a second. I saw my reflection and stared at it. Only three words came to mind. Goddamn screw up. That's what I had become. Or had I been that all of my life and had only recently come to see it?

Seriously, what redeeming qualities, or things to be proud of, or things to be satisfied with, did I have left? I wondered just exactly what my purpose was in life these days. To endure worthlessness? To bring trouble to others? At this rate I don't think I really brought happiness to anyone. Not one single person. What usefulness did I serve? I guess just to be a goddamn screw up.

I had never seriously contemplated the act of actually committing suicide but the idea it presented had crossed my mind from time to time. What did my life actually matter anyway? Would it really make any difference to anyone if I was gone? At this point in my life I didn't really think so. I was an insignificant speck of dust that didn't have a place to belong in the grand scheme of the universe. I didn't see anything on the horizon that would change that. I don't know, I just didn't see any hope for myself being happy. I continued to stare at myself until my mind went blank and I closed my eyes for a minute or two. Whenever I thought about my life for an extended period of time I would get this uncomfortable, heavy feeling in the pit of my stomach. I put my hand on the mirror and leaned on it for a few moments. I exhaled deeply before I left the room. Life was fucking miserable.

I was lying in my bed the next night just staring at the ceiling when my phone rang. Once, twice – I thought about not answering it. It was kind of late so I figured whoever was calling had a reason. I didn't bother to look at who it was and I just answered it. I heard a familiar voice greet me for the first time in a long time – too long a time. "Hey man listen, I'm sorry, we have to talk." It was Daniel Wells, my best friend in this entire world.

"You're right man. You know things got screwed up between us and we gotta fix it," I told him with hope in my voice.

"Yeah I've been an asshole lately and we can't not be friends. I'm gonna come pick you up in a little bit and we'll figure shit out."

"Just like we always used to," I added.

"Just like we always used to," he echoed. I suddenly felt like a prisoner who is granted parole after being behind bars for so long. It was late so I quietly grabbed my jacket and passed through the hall. I carefully made my way down the stairs, which still had the remnants of the bloodstains on them, went out the door, and sat on my front steps to wait.

Before long, Daniel arrived and I got in. I didn't feel awkward about this, as the situation may have called for under the circumstances. I just felt a little different, although I wasn't quite able to put my finger on it as to how. We pulled into the parking lot of a mini mall located near my house. The lot was completely deserted as all the employees had gone home long ago. Daniel turned the car off and proceeded to lean back in his seat before he spoke. "Hey man I'm sorry about everything. I shouldn't have blown up on you that night. I was drunk and pissed off but you didn't deserve that. I had no reason to be mad at you. The shit that happened with Tiff, I know you didn't try to do anything wrong."

"I wished it would have never happened," I answered back. "I mean, I feel so terrible about that. I don't know man. Maybe I shouldn't have even gotten involved in the first place," I pointed out.

"No, you were right in trying to be a real friend to her. And not just that night, but all of the time. It made me realize that I had to do more in my relationship. But I shouldn't have avoided you for so long. I was just mad and I was trying to spend time fixing things and dealing with crap but I shouldn't have left you hanging like that."

"Well it's not all your fault man. I mean, I made no effort on my part whatsoever. I could have at least tried to call you once to see what the hell was up. So what's the deal with Tiffany? I haven't talked to her either," I let him know.

"She was really embarrassed by the whole thing. She said it was immature for her to create all that drama. And about kissing you? She didn't know why the hell she did that and regrets it. She apologized to me, she wants to apologize to you but she doesn't know how to figure out coming up to you about it because she feels like such a huge idiot. She's really embarrassed."

"I won't make her feel stupid," I promised. I breathed out loud and then said, "Man, since then I've been really miserable. Like, a lot worse than normal. I've been drinking and smoking pot like a madman. You seriously have no idea."

"Like how much more," he asked.

"Dude I was bringing alcohol to school just to get me through the day."

"Holy shit. Dude what the hell?"

"I know. It's been bad. Just the other day I cracked my head open and had to go to the hospital."

"Wait what happened," he asked in disbelief.

"Well I was drunk and was going down the stairs in my house and fell head first into the railing." He shook his head incredulously.

"Are you kidding me man?"

"You wanna see it," I egged him on. I then lowered my head and pulled my hair aside. He took a look for himself.

"Dude…what the hell man? I want you to start taking it easy on all that crap. I don't want you to turn into some reject," he said, concerned.

"Eight stitches…a shitload of blood."

"Well I see you've been keeping busy lately," he sarcastically stated. It was the first bit of humor we shared in a long time. It was good that things were finally starting to get back to normal.

"So yeah, I wanna see Tiff and get back to the old routine between the three of us."

"Well things aren't exactly routine between us."

"What do you mean," I curiously asked.

"Me and Tiff broke up." Whoa! I sure as hell wasn't expecting to hear that. That was a major bomb being dropped.

"What the hell happened," I desperately wanted to know.

"Well over the course of the last few weeks we had a bunch of long talks. We ultimately decided that there were differences between us, things we might have too hard a time working out, so we decided not to cause each other any unnecessary pain. We don't want to hurt each other so we decided it might be best for this."

"Oh my God." I was floored. "I'm really sorry. How did it go?"

"We're still cool. It was pretty weird though, and sad. I think it's on pretty good terms though. The door's still open for us I think, if things should change in the future."

"Damn. That's crazy. Wait…did I have anything to do with this?"

"No don't worry about it," he reassured me. "This wasn't your fault at all. Believe me."

So it seemed as if life was continuing like some kind of steamroller. You can't stop it. You can't get out of its way. You just have to be ready for it and try to make the best of things because you don't want to get unexpectedly run down. I was glad to have my best friend back. I felt a comforting sense of relief wash over me as we continued to talk long into the night.

CHAPTER 29

Going to school the next day felt like less of a burden than usual. Now that me and Daniel were cool again I could at least have a little fun in the old hellhole. I decided to seek out Tiffany in the morning before school started. Even if she felt awkward about seeing me I was in possession of a secret weapon – a nice bagel with cream cheese. Her defenses would fall like a house of cards, heh, heh. I probably looked like an idiot wandering around the parking lot because I was unable to find her. It appeared she wasn't here yet so I sat on a handrail by the entrance to the lot.

When she drove by I gave a corny wave and a really stupid grin, signaling I wanted to talk to her and letting her know I was cool about things. Hopefully she could tell that I wasn't going to be holding our little incident against her. I followed her to where she parked and came up alongside her door, not doing anything except smiling and holding the bagel aloft. She got the message and rolled down the window. "Get in," she directed me.

"Hi Tiff. I have some breakfast for us. I missed you."

"Greg…what do you think of me," she asked.

"Huh," I responded, kind of confused.

"Am I the stupidest girl you know?" I was pretty direct with my words now.

"Don't start with that crap. I talked to Daniel, I know how you feel about what happened, and I don't have any negative feelings toward you. I understand you were confused or whatever, I'm not holding anything against you. I'm cool. And if you're really sensitive about it I won't even joke about it, I promise." She looked at me for a few moments but didn't say anything. Then she slowly smiled. Then she spoke.

"Greg…gimme some of that bagel," she playfully demanded.

"Cinnamon raisin – your favorite." After a few bites she spoke again.

"I really appreciate your attitude about the whole thing. Thanks for being so cool," she happily said. "I mean, I really screwed up. I don't know. I'm sorry. I really hope it's not weird for you."

"Don't worry about it." We sat there sharing our snack like two old friends. We were so involved with talking to each other and catching up on things that we almost didn't make it inside on time.

"How's the head, Madison," DeBurns asked me as I made my way into class.

"They said I have slight brain damage which prevents my…umm…neural cortex, yeah, my neural cortex from engaging in any mathematical operations for a while. Sorry to disappoint you."

"Well perhaps we can prove those doctors wrong Greg. I have the utmost confidence in your, ahem, skills," he sarcastically told me.

"I'm sure you do," I answered. I sat down and my buddy Paul frantically asked me, "yo man, you do the homework?"

"Kinda," I replied.

"Well pass that crap this way, I forgot all about it." I complied and gave him my copy of the worksheet to copy off of while the lesson went on. God, this crap was like a foreign language. What the hell was a polynomial anyway? I was just content to doodle around in my notebook because I knew for a fact that I couldn't master this nonsense. Yeah, doodling in my notebook and staring at Lisa, the girl to the side of me's, legs. I always heard she was a slut. Well if she wasn't she sure as hell dressed it, I acknowledged while being amazed by the shortness of her skirt.

"Ok, I'll collect the homework now," DeBurns announced as he made his way up and down the aisles.

"Yo dude, give it up," I told Paul.

"All right, one second," he said before eventually giving me back my paper. As I turned back around I noticed DeBurns looking our way. Gee, odds are he saw that. As he got closer to me he said, "Madison you're barely hanging on. I suggest you don't do anything to jeopardize what little chance you have left." He then moved on. I also heard him say some crap to Paul.

"Slick dude," I sarcastically said to Paul.

"Sorry bro." Math class ended and I joined the swarm of people in the hall, mindlessly walking to my next destination. As the day progressed so did my hunger. Well at least now my friends would be eating with me again.

I entered the cafeteria with Johnny and we encountered Daniel and Tiff waiting for us at our table. "Hey look who we have here," Johnny began in his crass but not really malicious way. "Where have you assholes been?"

"Sorry we haven't been around," Daniel answered.

"Me and Daniel broke up," Tiff explained.

"Ooooh. Is it me or did it just get about ten degrees more awkward in here. Crap," Johnny stated.

"It's ok Johnny," Tiff let him know.

"So you guys are cool? You don't hate each other," Johnny asked.

"No we're good," Daniel replied. After some more small talk we sat down to eat. The food was good today, not great, but good. Tacos and potatoes, fine by me. Things just about seemed to be back to the norm. This was the first time all four of us had been together since…damn it's been a while. Oh yeah, that damn party. Well hopefully the four of us never get torn apart again. I only hoped we remained as close after high school ended.

"So how does it feel to be the only one in any kind of relationship Johnny," I asked.

"Wrong there partner," he announced. "I'm not with Bethany anymore. I had to let her go recently." Tiff wanted to know what the problem was. "Why would you do that," she asked, seemingly not approving of the situation.

"I don't know. I was starting to get bored of her."

"You mean bored WITH her," I asked, trying to correct him.

"…No, bored OF her," Johnny reaffirmed himself.

"You are one shallow son of a bitch," Daniel laughed. "But what are you gonna do I guess, huh?"

"Live happily I suppose," he replied. Tiff then got up to go to the bathroom. Johnny watched 'til she was out of view before proceeding to take the time to acquire some key info. "Hey Daniel, did you and Tiff breaking up have anything to do with that Jessica girl?"

"Well it sure as hell didn't help," Daniel replied, annoyed, apparently remembering things.

"You still talk to her," I asked.

"No, I'm not that stupid," he let us know.

"So then you can help a buddy out," Johnny said with a smile growing on his face. "If you're not going to take her, give her to me," he said, as if haggling over the property rights of a girl was like bartering at a flea market.

"You can have her number but that's all I'm doing. I'm sure as hell not getting involved in this little plan of yours," Daniel emphatically spoke. I could understand where he was coming from. And with that Johnny got the information he needed. This was going to be an interesting proposition to say the least. Hmm, some days I wondered if Johnny was a dense idiot or a crafty genius.

CHAPTER 30

"You want to work in a factory Greg," my dad asked as he pulled his head up from the Sunday papers when I entered the kitchen. Well that was pretty random.

"Umm…"

"I talked to Stewart Murphy the other day and he says there are a few openings in the company he works for. Since he knows me, he can put you in if you want."

"A factory…" C'mon, I was an eighteen-year-old kid, not some peasant in the nineteenth century trying to provide for his family.

"Well you won't be doing as much heavy physical labor as some of the other guys," my dad continued, trying to sell me on the idea. "I mean, it won't be easy but it's something. You haven't had much luck in the meantime." Well that's because I kinda stopped looking for a job. Actually, I never really began. Crud, what choice did I have? I didn't see too much of a way out so I caved with very little resistance.

"I guess," I informed him. "So what am I going to have to do?"

"Well here's what Stewart told me so far…" my dad began as he took a generous gulp from his coffee mug.

It was six o'clock and I was just putting the finishing touches on my hair. Daniel and Johnny were waiting for me outside. We were going to see this local band play tonight. From what I heard, two of the members were graduates from our high school. I finished in the bathroom, went to get my jacket, and raced down the steps. You would think that I would have learned to go down them carefully, huh? I went out to Daniel's car and tossed myself into the backseat. "You finally ready princess," Daniel greeted me. The majority of the ride consisted of the three of us constantly insulting each other – a true bonding experience. You can't truly claim to know another guy well if you can't call him an ugly bastard or make crude and degrading comments about his mother.

After a while I had something observant to say. "Daniel, do you know where you're going?"

After a few moments of hesitation he replied, "Not really."

"Oh ok that's fine," I replied without missing a beat. I wasn't familiar with the town we were in but it had only been a twenty minute ride so it's not like we'd completely fallen off the face of the earth. "I don't think we were supposed to make that left turn off of Dominianni Ave.," Johnny said, giving his opinion. "I think we had to stay on it for longer."

"I don't know," Daniel answered. "I think I'll stay on here for a little bit, see where it takes us and see if we recognize anything." So we rode on. Nothing looked familiar to me. I hate being lost. I just can't handle the pressure and usually break down with thoughts of I don't think we're ever going to make it back to where we came from, and, gee I hope the car doesn't break down in this crazy ass place.

"Does anyone else notice that it's starting to look more and more ghettoish as we go on," Johnny asked.

"Yeah you ain't kidding," Daniel said as he overtly pressed the automatic door lock button. "I'm gonna turn back around." We all used our wits to help us nearly get back to where we had first lost our way. When we ran out of intuition we decided to ask for directions. There really wasn't anybody around we could ask so we started to get a little worried. We came upon some dudes who looked like they would rather steal our tires than give us directions so we asked as politely as possible. Surprisingly, they didn't carjack us or shank us on the spot so we repeatedly told them how grateful we were and then headed off on our way, able to breathe easy.

We finally arrived, for better or worse, at our destination. The parking lot was quite filled, as I'm sure we were just a bit late. I noticed the large amount of cigarette butts strewn across the parking lot. There were all sorts of people hanging out in the lot and near the entrance. As we were walking, these three girls passed us by. They were little punk rocker chicks who were probably a year or two younger than us. One had blue jeans, a Clash shirt, and short black hair. One had red pants, a Black Flag shirt, and blonde hair that had both spikes and bangs, which I liked. And the other had tight black pants, a studded belt worn low around her hips in a sexy way, a Ramones shirt, and had a lot of earrings and purple hair, which I liked more. They seemed to look at us as we headed toward the entrance. When we got in, the people in charge marked our hands to ensure we wouldn't be served alcohol. But yeah, let's give beer to the yahoos who were three years older than us. I never understood that logic. I mean, we could be trained as merciless killing machines and sent to far off lands to snuff out the lives of people we've never met before because Big Brother operates on its own agenda, but at the same time we're not allowed one lousy, stinking drink. Seems like some people have their priorities damn far out of order.

The band we wanted to see was already playing by the time we got in. They played some pretty basic punk rock music and seemed to be enjoying themselves. It was pretty cool that these guys weren't much older than us but were doing their thing here. And the crowd gave them a nice reception for their material but especially when they threw in some classics like "Blitzkrieg Bop" and "Anarchy in the U.K." They were a pretty enjoyable act and I hoped they would get far so that I could, in a way, vicariously live through them. I didn't recognize the drummer but I noticed the guitar player from high school. He was a senior when I was a sophomore. I didn't know him but I always heard he was a real nice guy.

Good for him and the other guys. Seeing these guys play gave me a little inspiration for us. The songs they were playing weren't blatantly difficult.

When they were taking their stuff down in preparation for the next act it was relatively quiet, so me and the guys had an opportunity to chill. I had noticed the black, blonde, and purple haired girls had come in a little while ago during one of the songs. Now, I had been discretely looking their way every now and then but I couldn't tell if they had been checking us out or if I was mistaken. Because after all, frankly, I sucked at this kind of thing.

While consulting my friends on the matter, the girls walked by the area not too far from us a couple times for no apparently legitimate reason. Daniel and Johnny agreed that they were potentially interested in us. I had taken quite a liking to the purple haired girl. I asked the guys what their take was but they were less than receptive. "I'm not interested in talking to any girls right now, sorry," Daniel said. "I just don't feel comfortable, it's too soon."

"Johnny," I asked.

"I'm saving up for my big plans over Jessica. I'm not too interested man," he let me know.

"You guys suck," I told them.

"You can still go over there," Daniel said to me. "If we all go over there you kinda have to deal with the factor of who wants who and who gets who. And that applies to both sides."

"I don't really feel like going alone," I said.

"Well which one do you like," Johnny asked.

"The one with the purple hair," I replied.

"Well if you go over there just focus most of your attention on her, they'll probably get the idea," Johnny advised me. This made sense, so after a good amount of cajoling by my friends I decided/was forced to go over there. I was damn nervous. I said something intentionally corny to get in and then tried my best to seem appealing. The girls were relatively polite and I wasn't made to feel like a fool, but then when I informed them that my friends were just here to watch the show I could sense their interest dissipate. I felt like I was getting the run around as Mrs. Purple Hair was trying not to hurt my feelings but I could sense that this was going nowhere. Rather than prolong the agony and awkwardness I pulled myself out of there like an animal that chews off its paw to escape a trap. I went back to my friends a broken and defeated man.

"Don't worry about it man. Next time," Daniel comforted me. I let out a deep breath.

"I'm getting pretty sick of waiting for next time," I let out, frustrated.

CHAPTER 31

High school was coming to a close in about a little over a month and I was uncertain how I felt about this. On the one hand, I generally hated the work, a good percentage of the people, and the rigid system. On the other hand, I appreciated the familiarity; I knew what to expect and when to expect it. This was what I was accustomed to and I wasn't sure exactly how well I would be able to handle some other endeavor. One thing was for sure though; I wasn't going to college, at least not at this point in time. I didn't think I was cut out for it. I was just able to keep my head above the water in this place. I figured college would kick my ass. And even if I changed my mind and wanted to go, I was already way past the deadlines. I just had my eyes set on graduating from this place, which shouldn't be a problem, barring some major academic blunder.

Life at the factory was new and interesting, which doesn't necessarily translate into good. That's not to say I hated it though. The company produced packaging parts. Since I was the youngest guy working in my area, the rest of the folks there kind of took me under their wings. They were relatively easygoing and treated me well. They were usually understanding if I ever messed up. With the machines running on the floor it could get hot as hell in there. I usually came home covered in sweat, it sucked. I wasn't in a position of too much responsibility; I usually did menial jobs. Lifting and moving things, cleaning oil spills, sweeping, putting packages and parts away and keeping them organized, and occasionally delivering messages between the offices and the floor. It looked like I would be spending my summer here until I figured out what I was going to do with myself.

"Greg, it's your turn," Tiff impatiently informed me.

"All right, all right." Time to refocus myself and nail a strike. Me, Daniel, Tiff, and a few other associates were gathered at Pinhead Alley, the local bowling joint that a lot of weirdos often hung out at. And yes, I was including us among those weirdos. I got up, approached the lane with my red bowling shoes that were a size too small, and picked up "Blue Thunder", my current ball of choice. "Ok, time to show you guys how a skilled professional plays those pins like a fiddle," I told my team before letting it rip. My ball showcased a mighty impressive curve as it reached its destination. Well, ten pins getting knocked down, four pins getting knocked down, what's the difference?

When it was all said and done, my team lost – but Tiffany did have the high score among everyone. "How did you possibly have the high score," Daniel questioned. "After all, you're just a, a girl," he said, comically disturbed by the situation.

"Correction, one hell of a girl," she smugly responded.

"I know," he conceded. The group then moved to the parking lot while trying to decide what to do. Victor, Steve, and Cindy, casual acquaintances of ours, had suggested bowling. They looked to us for the next plan.

"We could swipe some beers from Victor's. I don't know, maybe we could have some drinks tonight," I tossed out.

"Well maybe weee could have some drinks tonight," Daniel said, motioning to everyone but me. "You need to take it easy," he said before patting my head where the stitches were.

"No can do guys. My sister's home," Victor said. "Sorry."

"How about me and you drive around town," Daniel asked. "You're pretty proud of your Mustang. I'll go get my car. Just cause it's older than me doesn't mean it can't get the job done. We could race each other in different areas – highway, back roads, empty lot. Best two out of three. Let's see what my little Malibu can do," Daniel propositioned Victor.

"Yeah cause that's a good idea," he sarcastically replied. "I've gotten a ticket for speeding, I don't need to get in anymore trouble."

"A movie anyone," Tiff asked.

"No," most people responded. I wasn't much in the mood to really do anything else and no one could really agree on anything, so after a few minutes the group disbanded.

Me, Daniel, and Tiff went back to her car with nothing to do. "Hey I was here first," I yelled as Daniel opened the door to the front seat.

"Yeah so were the dinosaurs but that didn't work out too well for them either," he fired back.

"You don't have boyfriend privileges so you can't bogart the front seat anymore," I cleverly pointed out.

"Why don't you just shoot for it? Rock, paper, scissors," Tiff suggested. And with that we prepared to throw down. The first hand saw rock versus rock. All right, I have this in the bag. All I have to do is put down rock again; Daniel never suspects when I put down the same thing twice. Ok here goes. Ahh crap, the dreaded paper. I guess he had learned from his mistakes after all.

"Victory is mine," he proudly stated.

"Fine take the front," I said, and then in a lower tone, "you spoiled little brat."

"What'd you say," he asked.

"I said you're cool," while giving him a nice big smile. I had nothing to do when I got home and it wasn't really late, so just before I tucked myself in I took two shots of coconut rum. Not too big though, just a little something for taste before I went to sleep.

I was pretty busy the next day, as my dad needed help doing some work on the ceiling in his office room. After moving the computer desk and a bunch of other things out of the way, we were ready to put in new sheet rock on the ceiling. We hadn't hooked up the air conditioning yet, so as the day went on the late spring weather was really getting to us. I wouldn't say it made us lazier, just less eager to work. We were now sipping iced tea on one of our many breaks. "How's the factory," my dad asked.

"It has its ups and downs," I replied. "Some days are tougher than others. I got to drive a forklift last week though."

"Did you break anything?"

"Just my supervisor's patience. It took me a little bit to perfect it," I said.

"Uh huh. Ok, I guess let's get back to doing this," he stated while putting his drink aside.

I then spent the rest of the day finishing up a big English assignment. For the longest time I had considered tossing the assignment, but then when I finally found the proper direction for it, I found it surprisingly interesting. I had to choose a character from the works we had covered and after analyzing the character, describe how I had either something in common or was in conflict with said character. I chose Charlie, the main character from Stephen Chbosky's novel, The Perks of Being a Wallflower. I wrote about how the character's uncertainty and feelings of isolation and hopelessness and dealing with being an outsider really spoke to me and reflected parts of my own personality and experiences. But I really couldn't see any "perks". I enjoyed the assignment, just so long as after I got it back I didn't have to show it to anyone else and my teacher hadn't all of a sudden started thinking of me as a freak and need to put me on watch.

CHAPTER 32

Weeks had passed and a lot of people were starting to get excited about the beginning of the end of high school. You didn't have to look too hard to see the excitement on the faces of many of the seniors. And you certainly didn't have to listen too keenly to hear all the popular members of the senior class talking about – hmm, what did they like to talk about? You guessed it, themselves. For days they had been constantly jabbering about all their memories here. All the good times they had, how much they loved it here, how much they were going to miss this place, and how they would fare in a new school where they might not know anyone at all. Aww, well too bad. I guess now you won't have so many people around you to kiss your ass. Boo-freakin'-hoo! Let's see just how well you can handle the pressure of being in such a big place yet feeling so alone, huh?

So there we were in Johnny's kitchen discussing the immediate future. And one of the things in the immediate future, for better or for worse, depending on who you were, was the prom. The prom, the great defining social event of our time, was rearing its ugly head in a few days. I know I sure didn't have any plans on going.

"So Daniel do you have all the plans set for the prom," Tiff asked Daniel.

"Hey this is me we're talking about, what do you think," he responded.

"So…do you have all the plans set," she repeated.

"Yes, don't worry about it. I promised you a long time ago that I would take you to the prom and take care of everything and you would have a great time."

"Good," she said, happy that she was still going with Daniel even though they were no longer together. "So you're really not going, Greg?"

"Um, let me think about that for a second. No," I told her.

"That's too bad," she replied. "Why not?"

"Let me see. Maybe it's cause I have that dinner with the President, or that speech to give to Congress, or just maybe it's because, oh I don't know – I have no one to go with! That might be it," I told her.

"Oooook. I see you're being reasonable," she told me.

"It's the truth. What do you want from me," I argued back. She then shifted her attention off of me.

"Johnny, what about you," she questioned.

"Nope. I have plans. I'm going to be hanging out with the new girl," he said.

"New girl? Who's the new girl," she curiously asked.

"Um, I think you met her once," he slowly led in. "Her name is…Jessica."

"Oh yeah. I remember her," she slowly and deliberately stated. "Well it's good that you're gonna be occupying her these days." Daniel stayed silent. Then so did everybody else. I figured I would quickly break the silence.

"So what are you two doing afterwards? Gonna hang out with all the other promies," I addressed Daniel and Tiff.

"No I don't think so. We're just going to go back to my house and hang. We'll probably stay up all night doing something. Talking, or movies, or whatever. You can come man," Daniel told me.

"I don't think so. I'm going to have absolutely nothing to do all night. I don't think I have the sanity in me to wait all night like a loser for you guys to get back without first breaking down into a murderous rage or a catatonic state of depression," I grimly relayed. "Thanks for the offer though," I quickly and cheerfully added. "Don't worry about me, I'll figure something out."

"Yeah sorry man," Johnny came in, "But I need to be alone to hopefully work my magic. You know what I'm sayin'? Otherwise I would've bailed you out."

"Yeah I know," I told him.

"And I gotta go with my best tactics if I want to succeed because this is one grade A piece of meat we're talking about. Wait a second that sounded crude, even for me," he explained. "Let me rephrase that – one premium choice cut of beef. There, that's better."

"I think we all get it Johnny," Tiffany exclaimed. And then soon after we all went our separate ways home.

The next day I stopped by my old haunt, Rexmon's, to look at some boots. During the course of my perusing I got into an informative conversation with Chuck. I told him about my no prom attending ways and what he thought I should do to relieve my boredom. I asked him what he did when he had nothing to do. "Well when I got nothing better to do I'll take a trip or I'll gather some buddies and we'll hit the bar," he informed me.

"That does sound moderately satisfying," I told him.

"It's kinda cool I guess. Just so long as you don't go all the damn time. Then it gets kind of redundant," he explained to me.

"Well that's all well and good but it doesn't matter anyway. I'm not twenty-one to begin with."

"Yeah that does kind of suck," he so wisely observed. "Well what day is your prom?"

"Thursday, and then we have the next day off. They'd rather give us the extra day off on Friday than have most people not bother to show up on Monday," I told him.

"Wait, that's good. Check it, it's a weeknight. The bar I go to isn't a huge place. On weeknights they don't check IDs. Tell you what, on

Thursday I'll get some friends to go and if you walk in with us no one will even look twice at you. I'm sure you'll totally be able to get in," he claimed. I thought it over for a few seconds. What did I have to lose? This guy was being cool so I decided to take him up on his offer. I had nothing else to do anyway.

"Ok great. Thanks man, you're pretty cool," I told him.

"Hey I already know that," he said, smiling.

After a little more planning I let him know I'd meet him on Thursday. I then went and talked to Nancy for a few minutes before she placed an order for the boots I'd been looking for. "Ok Greg, I'll let you know when they come in," she said.

"Thanks. You guys are great," I said before turning to leave.

"All right see ya on Thursday man. We'll raise a little hell," Chuck exclaimed.

"Have fun Greg. And come back soon," Nancy said.

"Ok guys take care," I told them as I walked out the door.

Thursday came and I made one quick stop to check out Daniel and Tiffany. Ha, Daniel in a tuxedo was priceless. I made sure to get a picture because that was a moment that may never be duplicated. Tiff looked gorgeous in her red dress. If I hadn't seen it with my own eyes I never could have imagined her wearing something like that. The dress stopped just at her knees, revealing her black stockings and heels. I told them to enjoy themselves before leaving.

Later on that night I met up with Chuck and his friends a block away from The Golden Stone Pub. Supposedly one of the owner's ancestors struck it big mining gold, so sprinkled throughout the bar were several gold rush themed objects. Anyhow, Chuck introduced me to his pals Barry, John, and Matt. I said hello and then we started walking to the bar. Ok we're just about there, let's hope this goes smoothly. Opening the door, stepping in, no one asks for our IDs, bartender nods toward us politely as we enter, and there we go. Success!

It wasn't too crowded but there were a decent number of people in there. It seemed pretty cool, being able to hang in there and drink with no pressure. Chuck's friends were pretty cool, as they each insisted on buying me a drink because I was the new guy. I wasn't about to refuse and obliged them. They explained to me common courtesy practices such as tipping the bartender and, if it was crowded, offering your seat to any lady who approached the counter for a drink. "That's a good one," Matt pointed out, "Because you don't have to leave. You just stand near her and try to talk to her." John added, "It's good because you've already said something to her and established that you're definitely not an asshole."

"Yeah," Barry told me, "because you'll always have some guy who thinks he's some top dog and he's above everybody else."

"Most girls don't like that kind of guy," Chuck said. All this seemed to make pretty good sense.

As the night wore on I was getting pretty loose. I was having a good time hanging out with the guys when a few girls that they knew stopped by. The four of them ranged from decent looking to absolutely smoking. The guys introduced me and I tried my best to play it cool. The alcohol helped me to be a part of their conversation, allowing me to act as if I knew they wanted to talk to me. That was one of my problems. A lot of times in a group of people I didn't know too well, I wouldn't say much because I had a fear, which bordered on paranoia, in where I thought that no one wanted to talk to me or really cared what I had to say. Now, I didn't dominate the conversation but I did enough so as not to be mistaken as part of the wall.

When three of them went outside to smoke cigarettes the guys suggested I go with them. When we got out there they were polite enough to ask me questions about myself rather than just have a conversation among themselves. I feared I wouldn't be able to relate to what they were talking about and I would just stand there like an idiot. After a few minutes however, the entire ball of string began to unravel. After letting them know that I'd be finishing school soon they began to look confused. "Our semester has been over for a while now. What school do you go to," one of them asked. After informing them that I was graduating high school they smiled and chuckled in disbelief.

"Oh I'm sorry," another one began, "but we thought you were," she paused before smiling, "a little older." They weren't being malicious but I could tell from their tones that this was certainly not good.

We went back inside to join the rest of the guys and I could tell that I was now mostly an afterthought among the girls. They stopped talking to me as much as when they first met up with us, and I got the hint. This sure sucks. I forgot to take into account that any girl, at least one that hadn't snuck in, that I would encounter in a bar would be at least a few years older than me. I had a hard enough time in my own age bracket. I tried to comfort myself with a few more drinks before Chuck, who stayed sober, eventually gave me a ride home.

CHAPTER 33

"I need your advice man," Daniel implored me as we sat waiting for our food in The Grill Express.

"Shoot," I told him.

"I need to get Tiffany back. I really miss her man. Do you have any ideas?"

"Well first of all keep in mind that you're talking to a guy with no real romantic experience, so anything I say is just conjecture really. But I'll give you my opinion."

"All right. What do you got?"

"Well you should try and spend some time alone with her. Tell her exactly how important she is to you and what you'd be willing to do to get her back. I don't know."

"Well I think the prom helped work towards that. In a way I was kinda in the boyfriend role even though I wasn't. It would have been a lot more fun if you and Johnny were there by the way. There were some other people who didn't show up too. But anyway, we mostly danced with each other. Although, it did suck seeing her dance with anyone else, even if I knew it was just friendly, I guess since I didn't have the security of knowing she's mine," he said.

"And then what about afterwards," I asked.

"Then she came over and we just watched a movie and talked for a little bit, but not about anything serious. She didn't sleep over though. I figured she would have since it was late."

"Maybe you need to surprise her," I guessed. "Show her exactly how much you want to be with her. Do something romantic like you used to," I advised.

"Yeah. So what did you do that night anyway," he asked. Ah yes. I had something to trump him with now.

"Nothing really. I just went to a bar," I casually stated.

"What? How did you get in," he asked in disbelief.

"If you go on a quiet weeknight they don't card you apparently. I went with some dude I used to work with."

"Well how was it," he excitedly wanted to know.

"It was all right. His friends were cool and I did talk to some girls they knew –"

"All right Greg," he interrupted.

"No. No celebration. When they found out I was eighteen they didn't seem to want to talk much to me anymore," I explained.

"Ooh. That's not cool," he lamented as he finished his meal. We got up, laid a nice tip on the table, paid our bill, and quietly left. It was such a nice night that I could have just sat on the hood of the car and looked at the sky for hours.

I was awoken at 4:38 a.m. by a chilling dream. I was sitting in my car, literally out in the middle of nowhere. I appeared to be parked on a long, lonely stretch of highway. There was no traffic, no other cars at all. I was behind the wheel but my hands were down near my sides. They felt wet for some odd reason but I wasn't able to look down. I just sat there staring straight ahead. The only thing I could see were flashes of light that gradually became darker in color. I finally gained enough mental awareness to wonder why I wasn't going anywhere. I opened the door and stepped outside, still not looking down. My foot stepped into what felt like a puddle. I closed the door and was finally free to look around. I immediately noticed that a bloodstain covered the door and dripped down into the puddle I had stepped in. I looked at the ground and followed the drippings for about fifteen feet until I recognized my jacket on the ground. Alongside it was a bloodstained knife. I didn't understand anything until I looked down at the stained t-shirt I was wearing. I lifted up the shirt to reveal a sickening hole in my stomach. The wound was gushing and I started to feel weaker by the moment. My body then suddenly jolted awake.

What the hell was that? I was sweating and breathing heavily as I now sat fully upright in bed, wide-awake. That was one of the weirdest dreams I'd ever experienced. What was that all about? I suppose in the dream I had been stabbed. How that happened I had no idea. There was nobody else in the dream. Did I stab myself? Then I suppose I struggled to get to my car. Then I just sat there…to die I guess? What the hell did that even mean? I had no idea as I sat there looking out the window. I couldn't explain that one for the life of me. I decided not to even try. Finally, I slowly lay back down and just stayed still with my eyes open until I eventually fell asleep.

I thought about that dream just once more while I ate some lunch. Who stabbed me? Or did I stab myself? If so, what exactly did that represent? I considered dreams to usually have some kind of deep meaning behind them, explaining why you generated such an experience in the first place. Oh well, no matter. As long as it wasn't a premonition of my own death I'd be just fine. I tossed my macaroni and beef back and forth over the tray for a while. I didn't want any more food.

I sat at the table alone with Johnny because Daniel and Tiff or any other associates hadn't arrived yet. "So what's the scoop with Jessica," I asked him.

"We've been hanging out a lot. It's pretty cool," he excitedly responded.

"So you think she likes you?"

"I guess she likes me enough," he came back with.

"Did anything happen yet," I asked.

"I did kiss her once when we left each other. I'm not sure how much it meant to her though." How could a kiss not mean much to somebody? That was a foreign concept that I was still trying to fully grasp. "I mean, she didn't turn away or anything but I don't know," he continued. Unbelievable. Johnny had the nerves to kiss this girl? She barely even talked to me the couple times I encountered her. "I don't know what Daniel was thinking to let her get away. She's a ten for god sakes." Not that I wasn't happy for Johnny but for whatever reason I just couldn't get behind him as much as his excitement should have warranted.

"Well Tiffany is the girl for him. He was lucky enough to get her affection in the first place and I damn well hope he didn't screw up such a good thing," I declared.

Many hours later I found myself sitting with Johnny in his bedroom, tightly packing marijuana into a pipe he had. "This is the last of this stuff I have," I said. "I just want it to be gone. After I finish with it tonight I don't want to do it again for a long time. This shit is stupid really," I spoke.

"Ok pass the light," he said, not giving much credence to what I had just said.

"I'm serious man. Honestly, what's the point of this crap? It's not like it's really solving any of my problems," I truthfully acknowledged.

"So you're going to be one hundred percent clean from now on," he asked.

"Well, no," I had to admit. "Alcohol serves a function sometimes. But I don't want to go overboard and always be doing more shit than I need, y'know? I don't wanna become some burnout or alchy. So after tonight I'm gonna start toning myself down," I hopefully stated.

"Whatever you want to do man. That's fine by me," he stated. "You only have to answer to yourself." So I proceeded to mess myself up with reckless abandon, confident that it would be for the last time for a while and that I'd be clear afterwards.

Later that night, after I became a little more intelligible again, I decided to give Tiff a phone call. I wanted to try and put in a good word for Daniel because I'd rather see the two of them together than apart. "Hey Greg," she picked up. "What's up?"

"Hi Tiff, I just wanted to see how you were doing?" I was still a little goofy but it wasn't that bad. Certainly not suspicious or anything.

"I'm ok."

"That's good. Say, are you ever going to get back with Daniel," I blurted out.

"That's what you called me for," she said in lighthearted disbelief. "I don't know Greg. I want to but I want it to be right, y'know? Otherwise what's the point?"

"I think you should."

"Well I want to make sure I'm gonna be happy," she quickly replied.

"I think you would be," I said, continuing to be blindingly optimistic. "Have you thought about anybody else?"

"Well not any person but I just thought about the qualities I wanted and the type of person I wanted," she explained.

"Like what," I asked.

"Well I want to be treated like I'm the most important thing to this person. That's not too much to ask right?" I could have made several jokes but refrained and instead opted for, "No of course not. Nothing's too good for you doll."

"Ha ha, I gotta go Greg. I have to go pick up someone from work and give her a ride," she said.

"Ok. But don't decide on anything too quickly and without thinking about it for a while. All right?"

"I won't. Ok Greg thanks for calling."

"All right take care. I love you babe," I comically slipped in.

"Niiiiice," she responded before hanging up. Ok well the ball is in her court. I couldn't really picture them not being together anymore. And I guess deep in my mind I was a little worried about Tiff possibly slipping away. If she found someone new, he would be the most important thing to her. And then what? She would have less time for us, or for me. Would she eventually gravitate away from us? She was a good friend and I didn't want to lose her.

CHAPTER 34

"No, no. Slow down man, the drums aren't that fast," Johnny advised me. "They should be like half that speed."

"Ok. Got it." I had the house to myself so the guys came over to jam. We were trying to tackle a song by the band The Misfits. We went through it again for I think the sixth time, not having completed it on any of the previous attempts. After this latest collapse I saw Daniel slap his amp in annoyance.

"There's a repeat of the first riff dude," he told Johnny.

"I know. I forgot," he responded. We weren't doing very well. At least we had good humor about our suckiness however.

"If we can't do any of these songs we might as well sell our instruments," Daniel announced. "Except for me though," he added. "You? You guys suck, I'm great," he said, laughing.

"That's not what your mom said last night," Johnny retorted. A standard but quality comeback in any situation.

"Let's put the CD back on and listen to how it should sound again," I suggested. If we couldn't all be on the same page for a song that was barely longer than two minutes, where did we go from here? "Ok. Let's do it again. Daniel, turn your guitar down a little so it's easier to hear Johnny." After he complied I began with hitting my sticks together four times. We actually managed to make it all the way through this time. Well that was a start. "All right. None of us sucked too bad this time," I proclaimed. "We're improving."

"Great. Let's celebrate by taking a break," Johnny said.

"I'm down," Daniel confirmed.

"Me too," I agreed.

"Greg, fetch me a drink," Daniel demanded.

"You know where the fridge is." As he went upstairs I said loudly, "He's gone. Now we can talk about him," I sarcastically started.

"The only thing you queers are going to talk about is how sexy I am," he yelled from the top of the stairs.

While Daniel was gone we thought it would be funny to turn the volume on his amp all the way up to the maximum. Hopefully he wouldn't notice and when he unsuspectingly went to plug in and play it would blow his head off. Of course it would blow our heads off too but at least we'd be expecting it. Oh man, those sixty watts were going to be put to good use! Anyhow, he returned with a soda and plopped down on the couch. "Don't tell me that's the last Dr. Pepper," I threatened him.

"Oh, so that's what makes it taste extra good," he said.

"Damn, now I have to settle for the generic store brand crap. It sucks so much, why do they even give it a design? They might as well save money by just having a white label with black lettering that says Cola Product #1822 or something," I lamented. I got up to go to the refrigerator and instead of returning with an inferior product I settled on some water.

After I settled in we sat there terribly bored. Johnny was bouncing a tennis ball he had found down here and Daniel was using his feet to tap out the beat of the song we'd been practicing. No one was really saying anything to each other so I took the opportunity to accurately squirt a stream of water through my teeth and onto Daniel's arm. He responded by taking an ice cube between his thumb and forefinger and launching it into my leg. He got some pretty impressive velocity and it stung a little bit. I set aside my cup and the war was officially on. He had just enough time to put his drink aside as I rushed him. I jumped on top of him and a wild wrestling bout ensued. We eventually ended up spilling over the couch and decided to end it after we had both tasted floor.

We returned to our seats as if nothing happened. "That was pretty even but I'll give this one to Greg," Johnny declared.

"What," Daniel protested. But it was too late; the verdict was in.

"You guys wanna jam a little more," I asked.

"Yeah I guess," Daniel replied. Heh, heh.

"All right. Let's go," Johnny said as he got up. We took our places while keeping an eye on Daniel. Ok take the guitar out of your case, there you go. Put the cable in, then plug the other end into the amp, good. Don't look at the volume. All right, turn the power on buddy. The blast of feedback was ridiculous and it caused Daniel to actually stumble backwards before scrambling to turn it back off. Me and Johnny proceeded to laugh our asses off real good. I could barely concentrate on listening to Daniel's accusations or whatever the hell else he was saying because I was laughing so hard. So was Johnny and it only served to increase the intensity of my own glee. When it was all said and done and I regained my composure there were tears in my eyes and my stomach felt as if I'd done a thousand sit-ups. Good times indeed!

After practicing a little more, my parents came home and offered to buy pizza for dinner. I kind of wanted to blow this joint now but my buddies, not ones to turn down a free meal, persuaded me to stay. Thirty-six minutes later the pizza arrived and as per advertisement of taking more than thirty minutes we could have gotten it for free. However, the delivery guy wasn't much older than me and looked like he needed the job so my mom didn't hold him to the offer and paid anyway. It was a minor point of contention between my father and her that I believe would have been a slightly larger scene had my friends not been over. They were both stubborn and although they didn't fight too often, when they did it was a war of attrition. Since neither could actually convince the other party of the error of their ways the victor could only be determined by who had the endurance to maintain a high level of intensity all the way through to the end.

We gathered in the kitchen to eat. "So boys, how was the prom," my mom asked.

"I didn't go," Johnny answered.

"I went," Daniel replied. "It was ok. I don't know if it was a good enough time to be worth all the money I spent though," he declared.

"I'm sure it was a nice memory. Did you go with Tiffany, right?" my mom inquired.

"Yup I went with Tiffany."

"That's nice," she stated.

"So Johnny, I haven't seen you around here in a long time," my dad stated. "Does your father still work for that hardware company?"

"Yeah. It's a pretty solid job I guess. He's been there for a while now," he answered.

"And your mom," my mother asked.

"She stays at home these days," he replied.

"That's good."

"So, I like the nice faded red color scheme Greg added to the bottom part of the stairway. It gives the house a more fashionable feel. Maybe he should be an interior designer," Daniel joked.

"Oh my goodness, you should've seen it," my dad began. "I'm sitting on the couch reading something and I see him come in. When I look up I get a good view of him covered in blood and I almost have a heart attack for a second," he recalled.

"If you saw what it looked like you would have fainted," my mom added.

"Maybe you would have preferred me not to bother you and walk to the hospital myself," I sarcastically stated in between bites.

"I wish I could have seen it," Johnny piped in.

"Well it was something, that's for sure," my dad informed them.

"I guess we're going to have to change the carpeting on those steps. And maybe put a fresh coat of paint on the wall," my mom decided. After getting up to throw my garbage away I decided that we would be going. The guys thanked my parents and we gathered ourselves.

"Ok guys we'll see you," my dad said.

"Take care, and come back sometime," my mom added. The guys exchanged a few more words with my parents before we made our way out.

"All right see ya," I called as we made our way down the stairs and out the door. It felt liberating to finally leave my house.

The next day at school I got some pretty good news. My friend Steve, who was on the football team but was cooler than those other guys, informed me that he was going to be having a big party on Friday to celebrate graduation. He knew a lot of people so this would definitely be cool. It should blow Johnny's gatherings out of the water. "Aren't graduation parties supposed to be, you know, after we've actually graduated," I asked him.

"True. But I don't get to choose when my family will be away. Good enough? Besides, we should be celebrating as much as we can that we're finally getting out of here," he eagerly let me know as we slapped hands and went our separate ways down the hall. All right, this should be interesting.

Later on I ran into Johnny in the auditorium. "Yo," he greeted me with a suspiciously excited demeanor.

"What's up dude," I responded. After a bit of small talk I tried to get at whatever info he was keeping.

"I think I'm gonna be sticking around with Jessica. There's no way I'm gonna end up getting bored with her. She's the hottest girl I've ever been with," he proudly stated.

"How are things going," I asked.

"Pretty damn good," he excitedly responded. "We were making out the other night and she ended up going down."

"What? Are you shitting me," I disbelievingly asked. After he reveled in his own good fortune a little more, I'll admit I felt a slight tinge of jealousy. After all, this was one of the most good looking girls I had ever seen in my life. I just couldn't help but wonder why everyone always seemed to have such good luck. That is, everyone but me.

CHAPTER 35

"Hey man, what's up," I greeted Daniel as I answered my phone.

"You wanna hang a little before the party tonight," he asked.

"Yeah that sounds good," I told him.

"Hey I did it man," he happily began to inform me. "Me and Tiff are finally back together."

"Yeah? That's great man. Good for you guys, I knew it would work out," I replied.

"I'm driving now so you want to meet up at my house," he asked.

"Yeah I'll be there in a while," I told him before saying bye. Ok, so my best friends were back together. That's good news. I went to go get ready and took extra care for tonight. Made sure my hair was perfectly in place, took care to make sure my breath was smelling good, and even dabbed a hint of cologne on myself. You should always take proper insurance when preparing to enter the unknown.

I dropped by Daniel's and found not only him but Johnny and Jessica as well, hanging around outside. I said hello and acknowledged Jessica. "Greg. How have you been," she asked very nicely.

"Eh…I've had my ups and downs," I replied. We all talked out on the sidewalk for some time before Tiffany arrived. I guess we'd all be going to the party from here. I noticed Tiff give a side eye to Jessica when she went to greet Daniel.

"Hey babe," she said before giving him a good kiss on the lips. I wondered if she was trying to spite Jessica? Johnny and Jess were leaning both on his car and each other while Daniel was standing with his arms around Tiff's waist. I was sitting off to the side on some ledge. I was just thinking to myself now, not really saying anything. Hmm…Johnny and Jessica. Daniel and Tiffany. And me. I considered myself to be pretty out of place, like I just didn't belong here and now. I couldn't help but feel as if I were the fifth wheel. Well I tried not to look too out of place. I asked Jess a few questions for conversation. Throughout the discussion she gave us insight about life after high school, a fairly thoughtful thing to do. She was a nice person. When it finally came time to leave for the party, the group split up. Of course the couples left with each other in two cars and no one decided to come with me, as expected.

When I arrived on Steve's block I was amazed by how many cars there were. I had to go way down to the end to find a spot. Dang, this is going to be crazy. I'd never been to this guy's house before but from the looks of the houses on this street it should be huge. I didn't need to look at the numbers because I saw other people arriving and walking up his porch, inside. The door was open behind the screen but I rung the bell anyway to be polite. Steve opened up and invited me in. "Greg you made it," he shouted while giving me a high five using the hand that didn't have a beer in it. "Come in man. There's food in the kitchen, there's beer in the fridge, some guys brought a keg too. Help yourself to whatever you want."

"Great. Hey thanks a lot for inviting me dude," I told him.

"No problem. Just try to have some fun," he said before his hosting duties took him elsewhere.

Wow, there were a hell of a lot of people here. All types of characters too. A lot of Steve's football teammates were here, along with preppy guys, Barbie doll girls, populars, druggies, freaks, hip hop kids, and just about anyone else you could think of. I wondered what some of these people thought about the wide range of company. Who would have thought that freaks like me, Daniel, and Johnny would be hanging out at the same party as some of the most popular kids in our school? Hell, maybe later I'd have the audacity to go up to some of these people as if we were of the same breed. I'd love to go up to some of the most prissy and popular girls in our school and say what's up, just to see how they'd react.

Anyhow, tonight my game plan was going to be a little different. I was going to see if I could have a good time without really drinking. I was going to use my natural wit, charm, and magnetic personality to have fun, be cool, meet new people, and have a great night. But if that didn't work, screw it – I'd just get loaded like there was no tomorrow. You always have to have a Plan B. I found Daniel and crew but I wasn't going to settle on only talking to them the whole time. Tonight I was going to mingle and come away better than I came. The rest of the guys were already starting to hit the beer but I was going to hold off.

I made a swoop around the house, hoping to run into people I knew. When I did I would stop to say hello, have a bit of conversation, and see if I could use them as an in to help talk to people I didn't know. Things weren't going bad at all. After navigating through my associates I got the chance to meet some new people. No one too special as of yet but I did talk to a few new folks. This girl Hillary, who was into horror movies, Scott, who also played drums, Joe, who was simply a somewhat entertaining drunk, Amanda, who talked about her creative writing, and Walt, who was a basketball player. These people were all well and good but I hadn't truly connected to anyone yet at this party.

After a long period of time I migrated back to my friends. By this point they were all at various levels of intoxication. "Greg I missed you," Tiffany said while putting her arm around me and smiling.

"Aw, well thanks Tiff," I said.

"Next time you have to tell us when you leave because I was scared," she cutely stated.

"Sure Tiff. I will," I promised.

"Hey man, we should get you good and tanked so you can go talk to the cheerleaders," Johnny helpfully offered.

"Um, thanks for the help but I'll see what I can do myself first, ok?"

"So how are things Greg," Jessica asked. "Are you excited about graduating?" I told her both yes and no and informed her about my summer prospects involving the factory.

"Hey dude," Daniel began, "this is pretty cool. Are you having a good time? I want you to have fun and be happy. I love you man."

"I already know that," I told him. "You're my best friend bro'."

"And," he replied, not quite satisfied yet.

"And I love you man," I said.

"All right," he excitedly proclaimed. "Here Greg take a drink for cheers," he said before handing me my first can of beer tonight.

"What are we cheering," I asked.

"Us," he said while motioning to all five of us. There was no further elaboration. I guess it was that simple. He then lifted his can in the air and the rest of us followed suit. "Cheers," we all declared. I took a few sips from my beer but I didn't feel the need to finish it. I looked at my friends. To me they all seemed like moderately happy individuals. But me, I don't know. I just didn't seem quite fulfilled with myself at this point in my life and I was unfortunately beginning to accept it.

I got up and headed for the bathroom. I got to the door, which was about halfway between open and closed. Thinking nothing of it I went in. After closing the door behind me I was surprised to find a girl in there sitting on the floor against the tub. She sat there with her knees up, arms wrapped tightly around them, and part of her face pressed into the side of her arm. I was a little taken aback, first by the surprise of seeing her there, and then, more specifically, being amazed by how beautiful she was. I took her in from the bottom up.

She was wearing a pair of red Converse sneakers and a pair of black, very tight pants. Her studded belt hung down, hugging her hips. She wore a white and black baby doll shirt beneath her fitted blue denim jacket. The jacket was adorned with various studs, patches, and buttons, mostly relating to her tastes in music. A lot of the same bands I liked. She had an absolutely gorgeous face, striking me as somewhat cat-like if I had to categorize it. Very attractive. She had a few earrings in each ear and very light brown hair that had cherry red highlights in it. She had just a very small amount of black eyeliner on but that's where something was clearly amiss. It was all smudged around her eyes and a little ran down her cheeks. Apparently this girl had been in here crying.

"Oh I'm sorry. I didn't know anyone was in here," I said. She slowly looked in my direction but didn't say anything. "Hey are you ok," I asked, concerned.

"No," she quietly managed to say. Her voice still had that post crying quality to it. I moved closer to her and got down on one knee so we were just about on an even level.

"What's wrong," I asked. After a few seconds she responded, "I'm so sick of my life." Whoa, this was a little heavy.

"What's your name," I asked her.

"Stacey."

"Well my name is Greg. If you want you can talk to me, I'll listen. What's bothering you Stacey? What's wrong?" She looked at me and then looked down for a while.

"Nobody cares about me," she finally revealed. I sat down across from her so we were facing each other. "I'm not happy."

"Hey let me tell you something. I know a little bit about how you feel," I offered. "I was trying to forget about how shitty things were or how bad they can be. And I've spent a lot of time feeling sorry for myself.

But that…that's not good. It doesn't really help you and it doesn't change things," I spoke.

"I know but I can't help it. I feel so alone now," she said, her voice a little shaky.

"Why? What's the problem," I inquired. I hoped she would open up to me and I could try my best to help. "I don't have anybody. My parents – they don't pay attention to me. They're only concerned with themselves and their own bullshit. They spend so much time arguing with each other that they don't even know when I'm around, if I'm home or not or whatever. But I can live through that. But my boyfriend, he's the only person I thought understands me but he fucking cheated on me. I cared about him so much and I thought he felt the same about me too." Oh my God, I felt so bad for this girl.

"I'm so sorry. I know you feel really bad and I can't do anything to change that but if he cheated on you then he never really understood you to begin with, I would say. I know you can't just snap your fingers and make it better though. I'm really sorry. Here stand up," I told her. She hesitated for a second and then put her hand in mine and I helped her up. "Why don't you wipe your eyes," I said and gave her a bandana I had in my back pocket.

"Thank you," she replied. She cleaned herself up, including all the smeared eyeliner.

"I cared about him so much, or at least I used to. Is there something wrong with me," she desperately wanted to know.

"Well every person is different. Sometimes we make good choices and sometimes bad choices. He probably just made a real bad choice. Hey look in the mirror for a second," I requested.

"Yeah," she said, questioning me. "What?"

"Look at you. You're a very beautiful girl. Now, I know I don't know you but I'd be willing to bet you're just as beautiful a person on the inside as well." What I said wasn't some kind of sly play to move in on this girl. No, everything I'd said to her was really from the heart. I wanted to help her. She stared at herself for quite a few moments. I didn't say anything. I wanted to see what she would discover. By now she had regained most of the stability in her voice.

"Thank you Greg. You know, you're a very sweet guy. To get involved and everything. You could have just easily left me alone and walked back out that door. I really appreciate you trying to help me. Thank you," she said as she touched my hand.

"Well you looked like you needed help. What else could I do?"

"You're a good person," she said. "And I can't just let you leave now and never see you again. I feel like I should to get to know you more."

"Thanks," I replied. "I'd really like that because I'm sure you're a wonderful girl, Stacey," I told her.

"I really want to get out of here. Greg, can you walk me home please?"

"Sure. C'mon let's go right now," I said as I gently put my hand on her arm and led her out.

"Thanks," she sweetly replied. It took a mere fifteen seconds to get to the front door but as we walked together the moment seemed to last much longer. I opened the door for her and we both stepped out into the cool summer night.